Doctor Barre  **the bed.**

Lena couldn't help a strong awareness of his watchful gaze. Was he judging her methods?

"Before the birthing center, most of the mothers in Hickory Hollow had their babies at home."

"I was born at home," Ellen piped in.

Lena patted her hand as she folded the tape. It was kind of the young couple to defend her, defend the birthing center.

"I'm sure Doctor Barrett will come around as he begins to understand our ways."

If he didn't, well… He wasn't planning to be here long, was he?

His sharp eyes seemed to read what she hadn't said, and his lips curled slightly. In amusement? She couldn't tell.

She didn't need his approval. But she might need his help over the next few weeks, and she certainly didn't want him going around frightening every young mother in the community.

"We'll learn to work with each other soon enough, won't we?"

His answering smile was cool and held a distinct tinge of *we'll see*.

Lucy Bayer writes Amish novels from her home in the Midwest. She is a mother of four and an avid birder.

Books by Lucy Bayer

Love Inspired

A Convenient Amish Bride
Their Forbidden Amish Match

Visit the Author Profile page at LoveInspired.com.

Their Forbidden Amish Match

Lucy Bayer

LOVE INSPIRED
INSPIRATIONAL ROMANCE

LOVE INSPIRED®
INSPIRATIONAL ROMANCE

Recycling programs
for this product may
not exist in your area.

ISBN-13: 978-1-335-59859-2

Their Forbidden Amish Match

Love Inspired
22 Adelaide St. West, 41st Floor
Toronto, Ontario M5H 4E3, Canada
www.LoveInspired.com

Printed in U.S.A.

Therefore if any man be in Christ,
he is a new creature: old things are passed away;
behold, all things are become new.
—*2 Corinthians* 5:17

Chapter One

"Does Gramps know about this?"

Todd Barrett glanced out his side mirror, checking for traffic on the winding two-lane road. His brother Henry's voice was a little tinny through the Tesla's speakers, but his skepticism came through loud and clear.

"It's only six weeks," Todd said. "Not that long."

Up ahead, farms unfolded on either side of the road, idyllic with red barns and clotheslines hung with colorful dresses and black pants, cattle dotting the green fields.

Also up ahead was some kind of farm equipment spread across the entire road. Todd lifted his foot off the accelerator, relying on his tech-savvy car to do the rest and slow down behind the obstruction.

"Six weeks is a long time to take a detour from Gramps's plan for your life."

Todd frowned, but not because of Henry's words. The farm equipment looked like some kind of tractor attachment, with sharp wheels that would dig furrows in a field. A teenage boy in homespun clothes and a black hat led the pair of horses pulling it.

Todd couldn't see a way around. The tractor part blocked both lanes. A glance at the clock on the touchscreen at the dash showed he was right on time for his meeting with the local midwife. If he'd been home in Columbus, he'd have planned extra time in his commute to account for traffic. But this was sleepy Hickory Hollow. There wasn't supposed to be traffic here. If this kid didn't move off the road, Todd was going to be late.

He must've been mumbling to himself because Henry asked, "What was that?"

Todd grunted. "I'll be back in Columbus before Gramps even knows I'm gone." He crawled along behind the farm implement. A glance in his rearview mirror showed the road was empty. How far back had that last turnoff been? At least a mile. And there was no guarantee that it wouldn't lead to a ten-minute detour, not with the winding roads in this county.

"Was your new boss okay with you moving your start date?"

What was his brother's deal? Henry was pushing all his buttons today.

"He said he was." In so many words. Doctor Elliott, Todd's new boss, hadn't been happy about the delay, but he'd agreed to it. The emergency room job had been Todd's future since eighth grade, when he'd decided to go into medicine, like his grandfather and great-grandfather. He'd been invited to take the job after completing his residency at a smaller hospital across the state. The same one where his grandfather had completed his residency.

"I'm having supper with David and Ruby tonight." Todd changed the subject. "You should drive down this weekend and hang out with us."

Henry made a sound that might've been a grunt or a grumble. "I'll be in the middle of the Patterson job. Don't know if I can get away."

Todd didn't argue. The reason he'd pushed his start date back was a big one: last fall, he'd discovered he had a long-lost brother. David Weiss was Todd's biological brother and had been switched at birth without anyone being the wiser. Neil, the baby that Todd's parents had brought home from the hospital, had died when he was only a few months old. Todd had come here because he wanted the chance to get to know his brother and sister-in-law and their two young daughters. And Ruby was at the end of her second trimester.

When the local general practitioner, Doctor Bradshaw, had experienced a stroke and needed to retire immediately, David and Ruby and their entire community had been left without local medical care. Todd had agreed to step in temporarily. He'd met with the now-retired doctor this morning and discussed the caseload. Todd would be opening the clinic tomorrow.

And he was supposed to be meeting with the Amish midwife right now.

"I gotta go," he told his brother. "Come up on Saturday." *I miss you.*

Henry rang off without committing.

Scowling, Todd rolled down his window and waved his arm, trying to get the attention of the teen with the horses. It didn't work.

He didn't want to shout at someone on his first day in town. But he really needed to go. Every minute he wasted here was another minute he was late. Punctuality and efficiency were both key to running an efficient ER.

It seemed an interminable amount of time passed before the kid turned off into a field.

Todd didn't wait for him to clear both lanes. He sped around the rear of the implement in the left lane with a squeal of tires.

Doctor Bradshaw had sung the midwife's praises, saying that at least half the Amish families in town preferred to come to her instead of driving more than an hour to the nearest hospital. Todd had expected an office, but the Tesla's navigation brought him to a single-level farmhouse with a wraparound porch. Two empty rockers sat to the left of the front door. A small flower garden with sunny yellow blooms lined the foundation and extended around the corner. A black Amish buggy with a brown horse hitched to it was tied to a tree off the side of the house. A patient? Or the midwife herself?

Todd needed to work with this woman for the next six weeks. Doctor Bradshaw had said at least ten women in the community were thirty-five to thirty-nine weeks pregnant. Todd needed to make a good impression and gain her trust so they could have a good working relationship.

Starting out ten minutes late wasn't ideal.

He parked his car beneath a tree. As he strode hurriedly across the gravel in front of the house, his Oxford shoe squished into something. He glanced down and groaned. Strike two. The bottom of his shoe was now covered in horse dung. He glared at the tethered horse but it just swished its tail, unconcerned.

He detoured to the grassy area beside the house and tried to wipe off the nasty substance from his shoe. He could still smell it when he climbed the porch steps and slipped out of his shoes, not wanting to track it inside the birthing center.

He wondered how often such instances happened. What were the midwife's cleaning practices? There could be tons of nasty germs in a drop of horse poo. If her patients or their spouses were stepping in it and tracking it inside…? He didn't even want to think about it.

He raised his hand to knock when the door opened.

"Hello. You must be Doctor Barrett."

He stood in stunned silence, gazing down on the pretty young woman in a dark green dress and white apron. Her hair was burnished gold; he could tell even though it was tucked under one of those white caps Amish women wore. She had a faint spray of freckles across her nose and a warm smile that made his breath catch inside him.

He blinked, coming back to himself to realize he was staring at her.

"Are you Doctor Barrett?" she asked after he'd hesitated so long.

He cleared his throat. "Yes. I'm here to see the midwife. Lena."

There was something he couldn't read in her eyes. "I'm Lena. I'm the midwife."

Lena Hochstetler saw the warmth fade out of Doctor Barrett's eyes. Before she'd identified herself, there'd been the beginnings of a smile dawning on his face. She glimpsed the hint of disdain before his face went blank of all expression.

"You're Lena?"

"Ja." She managed the word along with a smile, but only barely.

It was only because he wasn't a part of their community. Everyone in Hickory Hollow knew her. She had been working alongside her *aendi* in the birthing center for ten years before her beloved *aendi* Carol had passed away. Three years had passed since and the grief was still fresh. Lena had her *aendi's* legacy to continue. Doctor Barrett wasn't going to be in Hickory Hollow long, so what did it matter if he was surprised by or frowned upon the fact that she was who she was?

It didn't.

Doctor Barrett hesitated in the doorway before he stepped over the threshold in his sock feet.

She might've been intimidated by him. He wore a crisply pressed fancy dress shirt, slacks with a crease pressed into them, and a stethoscope around his neck. He had a strong jaw and piercing blue eyes. He held his phone in one hand, and a fancy car was parked at the edge of her drive. He was very much an *Englisher*.

He was so different from Doctor Bradshaw that she would've been intimidated, if not for those socks.

He seemed embarrassed, giving a chagrined grimace. "I wasn't watching where I stepped."

Ah. "It happens."

And she appreciated that he wasn't tracking manure across the hardwood floors that she had mopped only this morning. Every morning, in fact.

"I don't have any new mothers in residence today. But I saw Jane Glick yesterday. She is thirty-eight weeks with her fifth child and was already showing signs of early labor. I will be surprised if she doesn't come in tomorrow or the next day." She forced herself to stop the flow of words, as quick as a babbling brook. She'd told herself all morning that she was going to be professional when she met the new doctor. And here she was, as nervous as a first-time father.

"If you'd like to meet one of my patients, she and her husband are here for a checkup." She extended her arm toward the back of the building.

"How old are you?" he asked. He shook his head. "I'm sorry. I know it's an impertinent question." But he didn't retract it.

Her smile stiffened as she led him across the homey living area, where fathers-to-be sometimes waited for their babies to be born. Beyond was a short hallway that led to the bedrooms she also used as exam rooms.

"I am twenty-eight." She'd surprised him with that statement. "I've been a part of the birthing center since I was fifteen."

She didn't owe him any explanations. But if they were going to work together, he needed to be able to trust her as well as trust the methods she and her *aendi* had developed over the years of practicing midwifery.

It was only the first day, the first few moments together. It wouldn't be so awkward again, not once they got to know each other. Doctor Bradshaw had been practicing medicine for so long in Hickory Hollow that he'd been the one to deliver her. He'd been a fixture, someone she'd known all her life. This couldn't compare.

Doctor Barrett was glancing around, and as they entered the hallway, his gaze caught on the framed drawings given to her or *Aendi* Carol by the babies who had been born at the birthing center and grown into children or even teenagers.

His eyes locked on the telephone hung on the wall in the hallway. He breathed a sigh of relief. "You have a telephone."

"It's how I call Doctor Bradshaw to let him know when he's needed. I suppose I'll be calling you now." She tipped her head a little to one side. "It doesn't happen often, but in some rare cases, I will have to call for a car service to take one of my patients to the hospital."

He was a few steps behind her as she put her hand on the knob of the first door.

"I think all babies should be born at hospitals."

She had already tapped twice on the door and was in the process of pushing it open when he spoke the words.

For a moment, she pretended she hadn't heard him.

"Ellen, Titus, this is Doctor Barrett. Do you mind if he sits in while we finish the checkup?"

Ellen Beiler sat on the edge of the double bed in the center of the room, reclining against a pillow propped against the wooden headboard. One of her hands rested on her rounded belly. Her lips were twitching as she shook her head. "It's okay with me."

Her husband stood to shake the doctor's hand before he sat back down in the straight-backed chair close to the window. The curtains were thrown wide to let in bright afternoon sunlight.

"Aren't you a bit young?" Ellen asked. There was no malice in her words, only curiosity. She must've heard him as he and Lena had come in the room. She had to be at least five years younger than the doctor.

Which was why Lena hid her smile as she turned her head to pick up the handwritten chart from the bureau against the opposite wall.

Todd cleared his throat and said, "I just finished a four-year residency. Emergency medicine."

"Have you delivered many babies?" her husband asked.

"A handful."

"Lena delivered both of our children," Titus said pointedly.

Doctor Barrett glanced at her, a flicker of surprise visible before his gaze went back to her patient. "I'm sure she's capable." His cool words said he was anything but. "But emergencies happen." To Lena he said, "You don't have the equipment or staff to handle a true emergency, do you?"

She'd checked the notes on her chart and placed it back on the bureau, taking a flexible measuring tape from her apron pocket. "In the case of an emergency, Doctor Bradshaw and I have always sent patients by ambulance to the nearest hospital."

"And if the ambulance takes too long? It's rural here."

Her memory bank provided an image of Dorothy, the young mother Lena had lost over a year ago. She blinked herself into the present and forced a smile. "Perhaps we can discuss logistics after I've finished my exam."

He should know better than to frighten a patient for no reason. Ellen had birthed two healthy babies and she was young and healthy and strong. She'd seen Lena for regular checkups and there was nothing in her chart to indicate she was at risk for complications.

"Would you lie back? Let's measure how this little one is growing."

Ellen complied, lying on the bed so that Lena could stretch the measuring tape across her belly.

Doctor Barrett stood at the foot of the bed. Lena couldn't help the developing awareness of his watchful gaze. Was he judging her methods? He must be.

Titus was one of the quietest men Lena knew, and she was surprised when he spoke. "Before the birthing center, most of the mothers in Hickory Hollow had their babies at home."

"I was born at home," Ellen piped up.

Lena patted her hand as she folded the tape. It was kind of the young couple to defend her and the birthing center.

"I'm sure Doctor Barrett will come around as he begins to understand our ways."

If he didn't, well…he wasn't planning to be here long, was he?

His sharp eyes seemed to read what she hadn't said, and his lips curled slightly. In amusement? She couldn't tell.

She didn't need his approval. But she might need his help over the next few weeks, and she certainly didn't want him going around frightening every young mother in the community.

"We'll learn to work with each other soon enough, won't we?"

His answering smile held a distinct tinge of *we'll see.*

Chapter Two

"*Onkle* Todd!"

Todd swept his niece Mindy off her feet as she raced across the living room to greet him. She hugged his neck with her little arms and warmth spread from his heart out to every extremity.

"Hey, munchkin. What have you been up to today?"

"What's a munchkin?"

Mindy's younger sister, Maggie, toddled across the floor, babbling baby words that he couldn't understand.

David, who had answered the door and was watching with a fond smile on his face, told his daughter, "Munchkins are a kind of character from a book. Maybe I'll read it to you when you're older."

Todd wanted to argue that she should see

the movie first, but the words died before they left his lips.

It was easy to forget.

His brother had been raised in an Amish family. They didn't own TVs. They didn't have electricity run to their homes, though they used battery-operated lamps and some gas-powered appliances.

Mindy probably never would see the movie with the yellow brick road.

Their lives were so different. He'd known it from the moment he'd first stepped into David's modest home. The house itself was well constructed and Ruby kept things clean and neat. But there was no technology. Not only was there no television, no computer and no cell phones, there was no telephone at all.

It was a little like stepping back in time to earlier days.

It'd taken him a while to wrap his head around it.

"Where's Ruby?" Todd asked when his sister-in-law was nowhere to be seen.

"She went upstairs to rest," David answered.

Todd's brows came together. "Is she all right? I've got my black bag in the car." He'd learned early on that carrying the bag with a bare modicum of medical supplies and tools was necessary.

Ruby was in her second trimester now, past the time when most miscarriages happened. But that didn't mean that something else couldn't go wrong.

David shook his head, a patient smile under his neatly trimmed beard. "I think she just wanted a nap after chasing the girls around all day. I'll check on her if she doesn't come down for dinner."

A delicious smell came from the kitchen. It always smelled good in Ruby's kitchen. Like bread and vegetables straight from the garden out behind the house. She spoiled Todd during his visits, often making cinnamon buns that were more delicious than anything he had ever tasted. His mouth started watering just thinking about them.

"How did you like the Schrock family?"

Todd squatted to see the crayon drawing Mindy had darted across the room to bring to him. Doing so also hid his expression from David.

"They were fine. Kind."

John and Denise had offered him a place to stay during his time in Hickory Hollow. The husband and wife couldn't be more than a year or two older than Todd. They had four kids ranging from twelve to five.

It wasn't David's fault that Todd's expectations were a little—a lot—different from reality.

Todd had been shocked to find out that what he thought was going to be a tiny apartment above an Amish grocery store instead was a single room. In *their* home.

It was as if he was stuck in an episode of *Little House on the Prairie*.

The room was tiny, dwarfed by the black leather suitcase he'd brought with him. There'd been a double bed spread with what he guessed was a homemade quilt, a small dresser and a rocking chair. It was plain. Simple.

And nothing like the sleek, brick and exposed beams apartment he had back in Columbus.

The Schrocks' entire apartment could fit inside half of his and he was pretty sure he'd taken a bedroom that belonged to the youngest two kids.

John had invited him to share meals with the family. Todd politely declined supper last night, claiming fatigue. Was he really expected to just…become part of their family for the next few weeks?

It was weird.

"My offer still stands. You are welcome here. We've plenty of room."

Maybe so, but he didn't want to wear out his welcome.

David and Ruby had only been married for six months. Todd loved being with Mindy and Maggie, David's daughters who'd been born to his first wife, but he'd sort of settled into his role as the fun uncle. If he was here every day, the girls might not think of him this way.

Especially when he spent hours glued to his laptop writing notes for patient files instead of playing with them. He'd gotten into the habit during his residency. There weren't enough hours in the day to see patients and write case notes. He didn't know how busy the clinic would be, but if Doctor Bradshaw's appointment book was as full as he'd hinted at, Todd would need the extra hours in the evenings to stay on top of things.

And he wouldn't lose his edge before going to his new job.

"Doctor Bradshaw showed me around the clinic today. I'll start seeing patients tomorrow."

"*Goot*. I know folks around here are glad to have a doctor again. You'll be just what they need."

Todd hoped so.

David had been the one to ask Todd to take over the practice until a new doctor could be found. He'd gotten the approval from the town council and found Todd a place to stay.

Their relationship was still new. And Todd really didn't want to disappoint his brother.

Ruby came down later and joined them for a delicious meal of white chicken chili and corn bread.

Todd leaned back in his chair, one hand on his full belly. "Can I ask you something?"

"Of course," David said easily.

Ruby stood and laid one hand on her husband's shoulder before she moved to the stove to fetch the coffeepot. She was barely showing her pregnancy at all. "I have apple pie," she announced.

Mindy cheered from her chair.

"Finish your food," David told her.

She frowned at the food still on her plate.

"Todd?" Ruby asked.

He groaned. "I shouldn't. I don't think I've got room for another bite."

It was too late. She placed a plate with a thick slice of pie before him. It was still warm. He could smell the cinnamon goodness as the apples oozed out of the sides of the crust.

"You really know the way to my heart," he said.

David chuckled, his fork poised to dig into

his own piece. "You need a *goot* wife. Especially if you're going to be working a lot of hours."

For some reason, Lena Hochstetler materialized in his mind's eye. The gentle way she'd examined her patient, the smile she'd shared with the Amish woman.

"Not a lot of time for dating right now," Todd said.

Ruby murmured something that might've been, "What a shame," but he couldn't be sure because her back was turned.

"What do you think of the birthing center?" he asked. He'd been thinking about it all afternoon, and not only because Lena had been about two decades younger than he'd expected.

And a lot prettier.

Ruby joined them at the table, serving a cup of coffee to David, who bussed her cheek with a kiss. She had a glass of milk for herself. "Lena is a *goot* friend. What do you want to know?"

"Are you planning to have your baby at the birthing center?"

Ruby and David exchanged a glance.

"We hadn't talked about it yet," David said.

"Most women in Hickory Hollow prefer it over giving birth at home," Ruby said. "Lena works hard serving the women, taking care of them during the birth and for a few days after. I've heard it's lovely to be able to rest and enjoy the time alone with the baby before going back to a busy life."

Ruby caught Maggie just before she tossed a handful of squished up corn bread over the side of her high chair.

She tapped the girl on the nose and stood up to start cleaning up the toddler.

She hadn't stayed in her seat long at any one time during the meal. Todd was surprised she'd managed to eat her own dinner.

He hadn't given much thought to it, but Ruby did have a busy life with little ones underfoot. And adding a newborn to the mix would make things busier. David's adoptive parents lived next door, and Ruby had a big family that lived across town, but having a few days to recuperate after a birth, spend time with the new baby without all the other busyness and expectations creeping in…

"That makes sense," he said slowly. "But I worry that a mother may have complications."

He shoved back the memory that wanted to escape the dark corner of his heart where he usually relegated it. He couldn't think of that now.

David considered him. "I think Lena has

helped birth enough babies that she knows when to send a mother on to the hospital. Is that what you mean?"

Lena had told him as much herself, though they hadn't gotten to finish their conversation.

He didn't know whether it was enough. And he'd taken an oath when he'd received his medical degree.

He might only be here for a short time, but he had a duty to see that every patient was safe and cared for.

And if that put him at odds with the pretty midwife, so be it.

"Didn't you meet the new doctor today?"

Lena glanced up from making the bed as her *aendi* Kate shuffled into the room.

"Yes," Lena answered.

Aendi Kate had moved in with *Mamm* and *Daed* last year, after her husband of forty years had passed away. *Onkle* Timothy had been a local carpenter. They had two daughters, but both had moved to Amish communities out of state when they'd married years ago. Emily and Madison, Lena's cousins, had both offered their *mamm* a place to stay with them, but *Aendi* Kate had insisted on staying in Hickory Hollow, where she'd been born and raised.

Aendi Kate's limp was more noticeable as she crossed the wooden floor to sit in the wooden rocking chair near the window. Six months ago, she'd had plantar fasciitis surgery on her foot.

"What did you think of him? The doctor?" *Aendi* Kate asked.

Lena focused on tucking the flat sheet beneath the end of the bed. "He was…" *Handsome. Focused. Arrogant.* "Young. A few years older than me."

She didn't give voice to her other thoughts. Not the way her stomach had pitched when she'd first opened the door to see him. Not how he'd rushed off after she'd finished examining Ellen.

"He may have a difficult time. Folks were used to Doc Bradshaw."

She'd thought the same thing earlier. Todd had seemed flustered when he'd arrived at the birthing center. Maybe that's why he'd seemed abrupt. Doc Bradshaw was known for his unhurried, laid-back ways.

Lena swung the quilt over the top of the bed, watching it slowly flutter down. She smoothed it with both hands before moving to tuck it in at the foot of the bed.

"He won't be in town for long," Lena said.

That's what she'd told herself when Todd had

hurried out of the birthing center, and she'd been left in the quiet, feeling as if something was missing.

"Doc Bradshaw will find another doctor to take over the clinic permanently."

Aendi Kate harrumphed, staring out the window at the darkening sky. Lena had been so focused on her task of making the bed that she hadn't noticed the faint lines of pain around her *aendi's* mouth until now.

"Want me to rub your foot?" she offered.

Aendi Kate shrugged, but she didn't say no.

Lena folded herself onto the floor at her *aendi's* feet, arranging her skirts around her legs. She brought Kate's foot forward to rest on her knee and began massaging her ankle and lower calf.

Some of the tightness left *Aendi* Kate's expression. She must've been in pain. Poor Kate.

"You're a *goot* girl, Lena. A credit to your *mamm.*"

Lena took the praise and tucked it into her heart.

Mamm didn't often utter words of praise. At least, not to Lena. But she'd been the one to suggest Lena help *Aendi* Carol at the birthing center when Lena had been a teenager. If it weren't for *Mamm*, Lena wouldn't have found her calling.

Lena lived in the small back bedroom at the birthing center. The same room *Aendi* Carol had lived in for thirty-six years before she'd died. But once a week, she walked or biked the two and a half miles to have supper at *Mamm's* table.

Tonight at the supper table, *Mamm* had mentioned that Kate's room needed refreshing and asked Lena to stay after supper to help.

Lena was glad to do it. But that meant that her own chores at the birthing center would be waiting for her when she got home.

Family was important. Of course she'd stayed.

After a few minutes of ministrations, *Aendi* Kate had grown more relaxed.

"Your cousin is getting married," she said suddenly.

Lena's heart panged for a prolonged moment. When she could trust her voice to emerge even, she asked, "Which one? Penny?" Lena had a dozen cousins. Only a couple were unmarried.

"Penny," *Aendi* Kate confirmed.

It wasn't a surprise. Penny was almost twenty now, and she'd been spending time with a serious young man named Jeb for a long time. As many young Amish couples did, they'd kept their relationship quiet, but the family had speculated whether they would get married this year.

"That's *goot*," Lena said. She smiled calmly when *Aendi* Kate's sharp gaze narrowed on her face. "I'm happy for her."

It wasn't a lie. Lena was happy for her cousin. Penny wasn't the first member of their family who was younger than Lena to marry.

It'd been Lena's younger sister Julie first, and then cousins Marybeth and Molly.

Now it was Penny's turn.

"I'll have to start embroidering some napkins." It was the gift she usually gave at family weddings.

Aendi Kate kept her probing gaze on Lena for longer than was comfortable before sighing.

"My foot is better now."

Lena stood up from the floor, glancing around the room with critical eyes that were a benefit when she prepared rooms at the birthing center to host new patients. The bed was made, the floor swept, the clutter on top of the dresser straightened. It was perfect.

"I'd better get home," she murmured. It would already be dark by the time she rode her bicycle there.

She hugged her *aendi* and then did the same for *Mamm* and *Daed* downstairs.

It was only when she was safely in her own room that she pressed her face into her pillow and cried.

She didn't begrudge Penny her happiness.

But once upon a time, Lena had dreamed of having a family of her own. A husband to love and who loved her in return. Children to fill a house and maybe even a dog.

Lena isn't the marrying type.

The old words played in her memory. The old hurt rose to choke her with new tears.

It had been more than ten years, but the words still had power to slice her open inside. She'd been sixteen, still full of hopes and expectations.

Until she'd overheard her *mamm* and one of *Mamm's* close friends, Samantha Prentice talking in the kitchen. Lena had hung back in the hallway, just outside, when she'd heard her name.

"Do you think Lena has a secret beau?" Samantha had asked. Lena heard the clink of a *kaffee* mug against the table.

"*Ach*, no." *Mamm's* quick answer had pinched a little. Sometimes, especially when a relationship was new, Lena's friends kept it a secret, even from their families. But *Mamm* had dismissed the idea of Lena having a beau so *quickly*.

"She's…"

Whatever Samantha had been about to say was cut off by *Mamm's* brisk words. "She isn't like her sisters. Lena isn't the marrying type. It's why I've been sending her over to help Carol. Lena would do well to have a job."

Because she won't marry.

Lena had slipped away, desperately hurt by the snippet of conversation she'd overheard. She knew she wasn't as pretty as her sisters. Vanity was a sin and Amish girls weren't supposed to primp or focus on their beauty.

But anyone with eyes could see that Lena's face was rounder than her sisters'. She'd always thought her hair was a drab light brown and her features weren't arranged in a pleasing way like many other girls.

She'd thought none of that mattered, but she'd been wrong.

Mamm had never said anything to her outright, but Lena had not forgotten that overheard conversation. A few months later, Lena had stopped waiting in breathless anticipation for one of the boys at the singings or at house church to notice her, to ask her to go walking or on a buggy ride. And after John Riehl rejected her, she'd given up.

She'd found solace in the busy work at *Aendi*

Carol's birthing center. A sense of purpose. She'd never quite gotten up the courage to ask why *Aendi* Carol had never married, but she'd come to believe they were the same. Both spinsters meant to help women and their babies.

She loved the work she did. She wouldn't know who she was without it.

But on a night like tonight, when she had to face the fact all over again that she would never have her childhood dream of a husband and a family, she couldn't hold her tears inside.

Chapter Three

"Good morning, Harold. Good morning, Amos."

Todd's ears perked up from the exam room at the very back of the clinic. It was still early, thirty minutes before the posted hours for opening. He'd arrived forty-five minutes ago and was getting the rooms prepped for the day.

He had expected Mrs. Smith, the office manager Doctor Bradshaw had introduced him to yesterday, to arrive at least half an hour ago. Maybe that was her now. But who was she greeting? No one should be inside.

He strode from the back of the clinic to the small waiting room with the receptionist desk. He was surprised to see Lena, along with two older men who had been sitting on the wooden bench outside the clinic this morning. The clinic was on Main Street and he'd nodded a hello to the gentlemen as he'd entered. He'd figured they must like to sit out and watch the town wake up.

They shuffled into the waiting room and sat in two of the wooden chairs.

Lena caught Todd's glance from where she was messing with the coffeepot set up on a small table across the room. He hadn't even thought of brewing coffee yet. His grumbling stomach had sent him downstairs to have breakfast with the Schrock family. He'd been plied with bacon and eggs and strong coffee and nonstop questions from the ten-year-old son, Joseph, about living in the city.

"Good morning, Doctor," Lena said.

"…Good morning. What are you doing here?"

She ignored his question, her attention on the ground coffee she was adding to the machine. "Meet Harold and Amos Glick. These two brothers have lived in Hickory Hollow all their lives."

He moved to shake their hands.

"Are you here to see me?" he asked.

One of the men—Amos, he thought—looked cross. "Not sure whether we want to, since you didn't see fit to let us in when you walked by."

The other brother coughed slightly. "Locked the door right behind you."

Todd was taken aback at their directness and cleared his throat. "The clinic's hours are posted on the door."

Lena bustled past him to offer both men a Styrofoam coffee cup filled with water. "Coffee will be ready in a few minutes."

She tipped her head to Todd, a clear directive. He followed her toward the receptionist desk. She spoke quietly. "Doctor Bradshaw usually opened the doors when he arrived. If there was anyone waiting, he would see them even if it was outside of his official hours."

Todd frowned.

He was opening his mouth to ask her how the man kept his clinic stocked and sanitized if he saw patients at all hours, but she was already speaking again. "Harold and Amos are pillars of the community. It would be a good thing for you to see them. Do you have an exam room ready?"

He didn't appreciate being pushed around by the petite midwife. But it wasn't like he could argue with her with the two men sitting right there.

"What are you doing here?" he asked Lena again.

"Mrs. Smith wasn't feeling well this morning. She sent over her son to ask whether I could help out in the clinic today."

"You don't have any patients of your own?"

"Not today. Not unless Jane Glick—Amos's granddaughter—goes into labor."

He felt his brows crinkle. "And if she does?"

"I left a note on the front door. They can phone over here and find me."

He was relieved that she had a process. "So you helped Doctor Bradshaw often?"

"Occasionally."

The smell of percolating coffee was starting to fill the waiting room and overpower the antiseptic scent.

The front door opened. A glance at his smartwatch showed it wasn't time for the clinic to be open yet, but a mother in an Amish dress and apron and two boys that looked to be about ten and twelve traipsed inside and sat down.

"Good morning," Lena said with a warm smile.

She hadn't smiled at him like that.

At this rate, he was going to have a full waiting room well before opening time.

"I suppose I'd better see them," he said on a sigh. "Bring one of them back?"

He strode to the back of the clinic, where Doctor Bradshaw had a small office. The man hadn't cleaned out his space, after his stroke and quick retirement. One entire wall was filled with floor-to-ceiling bookshelves crammed with medical texts. When Todd had glanced at them, he'd been surprised to see books with copyright dates of twenty and thirty years ago. Things had changed a lot in the medical profession during those years. He hoped Doctor Bradshaw had kept up on his continuing education.

Putting on the white coat he'd laid out neatly over the chair behind the desk, he slipped his stethoscope into his pocket and a small hammer with rubber ends into the other. There wasn't time to consult the patient records today. He didn't know if he'd have time even to see the patients on the paper schedule behind the receptionist's desk.

He had been shocked to discover that Doctor Bradshaw had no computerized records. Bradshaw had a longhand file for each patient. Some of them were badly out-of-date. The old doctor either was overworked or lazy and hadn't finished them.

Todd met Lena in the hallway, holding his laptop in hand. Her eyes widened as she took in his appearance. But rather than commenting she held open the door to the exam room.

He walked inside and found both brothers sitting on chairs. One of them whistled.

The other smirked. "You didn't have to get all gussied up for us."

Todd held back a retort. There was nothing wrong with wanting to look professional. In the city, what he was wearing might've even been considered too casual. He didn't have on a tie with his dress shirt. And these were khakis, not slacks.

"We have three exam rooms," he said. "I can see you separately. If you both stay here, there won't be any patient confidentiality."

The brothers exchanged a glance. Amos spoke. "We've lived a hundred feet from each other since I married my Wilma. Fifty-five years now. We don't have any secrets from each other."

Harold shrugged.

Todd glanced down at his laptop screen. Of course it was blank. He set it on the counter along one wall. "I'm not up to speed on Doctor Bradshaw's record. Would you like to tell me what's going on? Who wants to go first?"

Harold crossed his arms over his chest, a stubborn look coming over his face. "I told you we shouldn't have come. The fancy-pants doctor here isn't going to be able to help us like Doc Bradshaw could."

Todd bristled. The man hadn't even given

him a chance. It wasn't his fault he didn't know about Doctor Bradshaw's bad habit of opening the doors early or that he'd have patients waiting outside.

Lena touched his arm, shocking him enough to realize how tense he'd grown. He took a breath and forced himself to relax.

Before he could say anything, Lena spoke. "Doctor Barrett is an excellent physician. He came highly recommended from the hospital where he completed his residency and was top of his class."

He hadn't expected her to come to his defense. He schooled his expression as she looked straight at him.

"Harold has bad gout and I'm guessing by the way he keeps shifting in that chair that he's having a flare-up. Amos has high blood pressure and probably needs a refill on his medication."

He didn't know why she was helping him. Not after he'd questioned her yesterday at the birthing center. Maybe she only wanted to help the two men.

She held out a blood pressure cuff toward him, wearing an expectant look.

At this moment, she was his ally. "You'd better call me Todd," he murmured as he reached for it.

* * *

The morning was busy, and Lena was kept on her toes as they saw patients. Most people responded to Doctor Todd the same way that Harold and Amos had, with thinly veiled suspicion.

He was an outsider. An *Englisher.*

Doc Bradshaw had been an outsider, too. But that had been forty-five years ago, when he'd established his practice. He often reminisced and jokingly said that it'd taken him a good decade to earn his patients' trust.

Todd didn't have decades. He would only be here for six weeks.

And so she was stuck in the middle. Everyone knew her. And she knew most everyone's medical complaints and her way around the clinic.

"Is it always this busy?" Todd asked during a brief reprieve midmorning.

The waiting room had emptied, and they'd both retreated to the tiny kitchen slash storage room sandwiched between the furthest exam room and Doc Bradshaw's office.

"No. There are busy days, of course. But these families have been without medical care for weeks now."

She knew how days like this could go, so she had pulled her lunch out of the fridge. Her ham sandwich on homemade bread, macaroni salad and apple slices had never looked so appetizing.

She caught Todd's glance before he turned his back and went to the faucet to fetch a glass of water.

"You've been a big help today," he said. "I'm grateful."

What did it say about her that such a casual compliment made her blush?

She turned her face down to take a bite of her sandwich. The thick-sliced ham and bite of spicy cheese burst across her tongue. She leaned her hip against the table and paper crinkled from the pocket in her dress. She'd gotten a letter from one of her out-of-state cousins and stuffed it and the rest of the day's mail in her pocket as she'd left. She would read it later.

"How did you know that stuff about me?" He seemed almost bashful as he asked.

She could see in her mind's eye his surprised and contemplative expression when she'd told Harold and Amos about his experience.

Now he shook his head with a chagrined laugh. "If we were standing in a hospital in Columbus, I'd guess you stalked me online. Looked me up on social media," he said when she must've looked as perplexed as she felt.

She'd seen *Englishers* with their noses glued

to their phones. Knew that there were ways you could look up people on the internet. But no, she'd never done that before.

"Doc Bradshaw told me when he mentioned you would be working here temporarily. I think he wanted to reassure me that you'd be a good partner when it's time for us to work together."

The skin around his eyes tightened minutely before he smoothed his expression. His eyes darted to her sandwich again then quickly away.

"Here." She picked up the half she hadn't bitten yet and offered it to him.

"No, I'm—" His stomach growled audibly, and he sighed and ran a hand down his face. "Okay, thank you." He took it from her and bit into it, groaning with delight at the first taste.

She hid a grin by taking a drink of her own water, then sat at the small table to give her feet a few minutes' rest. "Doc Bradshaw usually brought his own lunch."

"Yeah, I—" He laughed a little. "I didn't expect things to be so...old-fashioned, I guess?" He chewed and swallowed. "I mean, I've visited David and Ruby a lot over the past months. But I never noticed that there wasn't a fast food joint in town. I usually grab lunch at the hospital cafeteria."

"Mrs. Schrock would probably be glad to make your lunch before you leave for the day."

He pulled a face. Apparently, that wasn't an answer he wanted to consider.

"Or the restaurant could make you a to-go order and have someone run it over."

That idea made his eyes light up. "Maybe I'll do that. Tomorrow. Thank you for the sandwich." He raised the last bite like a salute before he popped it in his mouth.

The bell on the front door jangled, and Todd turned to the sink and began to wash his hands. When she would've stood up, he waved her off. "Finish your lunch. I'll be fine without you. For a few minutes, at least."

He shot a smile at her before he went out the door, and she slumped back in her chair, heart racing.

Todd had seemed much more relaxed these past few minutes as they'd shared her lunch. More approachable. His smile had come more easily.

Why didn't he show that side of himself to his patients? Once he stepped foot in an exam room, he was no-nonsense and almost ruthless in his efficiency. His manner was brusque and he didn't make small talk with anyone.

If he had, maybe the patients he'd seen today would've taken more of a liking to him.

She liked him.

And it was a little silly, because nothing could come of it. He was an *Englisher* and planned to leave in only a few weeks.

Not that he would have any personal interest in her. She didn't kid herself that the appreciative glances she'd been receiving this morning were anything about her looks or being with her. Todd simply was glad to have someone to help him with difficult patients and a busy morning.

Lena isn't the marrying kind.

She needed to silence her out-of-control thoughts and quickly fished her mail out of her pocket. Cousin Bella's letter would be a nice distraction.

But she noticed an envelope on top of the letter first. It had an official crest from the state hospital board. She'd never received an official letter like this. To her knowledge, *Aendi* Carol hadn't, either.

Curiosity gave way to dismay as she opened the flap and read the letter.

We have no record of your hospital registration. The Hickory Hollow birthing center is out of compliance and must cease operations effective immediately.

What?

She reread the letter, but it still didn't make any sense. *Aendi* Carol had never told her about registering with the county. As far as Lena knew, the birthing center was operated as a small, home-based business. She paid taxes. Kept meticulous records.

This had to be a mistake.

Her heart was pounding with a rush of useless adrenaline. The birthing center couldn't be closed. Several mothers were planning to stay with her during the next few weeks, and even more who were pregnant would need her services in the coming months.

This was *Aendi* Carol's legacy and now Lena's.

She must find a way to resolve this.

Chapter Four

Todd's cell phone buzzed from the console beneath the wide computer screen in his car. The country road he was driving on was empty and he was going slow enough that he couldn't resist letting his gaze flick down to the phone screen. It was a text from *Dad*. Probably following up on their conversation this morning about his dad's last test results from a follow-up to the heart problem he'd experienced last year. Todd would have to check it later.

"Didn't you have time to eat lunch today?" Ruby asked.

Todd realized belatedly that his stomach was rumbling. It was noticeable in the quiet of the car, because the girls weren't present. David's mother was watching them.

His sister-in-law was in the front passenger

seat. It was an incongruent picture, her in her home-sewn dress and prayer *kapp* in his technology-rich car. The Amish people in Hickory Hollow followed the tradition of not owning cars of their own, but there was no rule against them riding in an automobile if needed.

He blinked away those thoughts and reminded himself of her question.

"Not too busy. I forgot to stop by the restaurant and ask them to send me something at lunch." And he hadn't wanted to leave the clinic, even to walk across the street, in case someone came in with a medical emergency.

He was beginning to wonder if coming to Hickory Hollow hadn't been a mistake.

After the first few days of back-to-back patients from morning until evening, visitors to the clinic had tapered off.

Today he'd seen all of three patients.

"I'm sure Mrs. Schrock would pack you a lunch," Ruby said. Lena had suggested as much.

He gave a noncommittal hum at that. The family he was staying with was kind enough, but he didn't want to be a burden. Didn't want to ask for too much. They were already housing him free of charge.

"I'd prefer to see to my own lunch," he said.

"But you didn't see to it."

He glanced at his sister-in-law. Her eyes were on him and she wore a hint of a smile, even though her words reminded him of Mindy. The girl could be quite persuasive—just on the edge of being argumentative—when she wanted her way.

Before this moment, Todd wouldn't have said Ruby could be the same. She was sweet and kind. He hadn't spent much time with her without David and the girls present. Was she naturally stubborn?

Yesterday, David had stopped by the Schrocks' home after supper to ask Todd if he'd bring Ruby to see the midwife this afternoon. Todd had almost asked him why he hadn't just texted the request.

It still hadn't sunk in—or maybe it just seemed so strange that Todd had trouble fathoming it—for the Amish people here to live without the conveniences that Todd found necessary.

Yesterday, David had taken an extra hour out of his day, driving his horse and buggy two miles out of the way to ask Todd a simple question. A text message would've taken thirty seconds.

But maybe Todd was thinking about things incorrectly. He should be honored that David had asked him to bring Ruby to this appointment when he could've just asked his adoptive father to hitch their buggy and bring her.

Todd pulled his car into the wide graveled area in front of the birthing center. He tapped the button to put the car into Park and then held on to the steering wheel as he stared at the structure.

A buggy was parked in front of the birthing center.

He probably should've come out here again. He hadn't seen Lena since the day she'd helped out at the clinic last week. They'd gotten along all right. She was proficient in the exam rooms and seemed to know everyone by name and quite a bit about each person.

Mrs. Smith had come back that second day. Todd didn't think the office manager was as personable as Lena. Or maybe she didn't like him.

Lena was supposed to call Todd if one of the young mothers went into labor. But how did he know whether she would call early enough? He still didn't appreciate the idea of the birthing center. A hospital would be better.

"You'll have to help me out of here." Ruby was poking at the passenger door.

"It's just that button. There." Todd pointed and she managed to get the door open.

Todd liked the way the doors popped open themselves at the push of a button.

He followed Ruby across the yard to the door and inside. She hadn't knocked.

"I'll be right with you." That was Lena's voice, slightly muffled as she called out from inside the first exam room down the hallway.

He wondered which young mother she was seeing. There'd been one visibly pregnant woman who'd visited the clinic last week, though she'd been there on behalf of her toddler son.

It would be great if Lena would introduce him to all her patients. She had such a winning way with people.

His phone buzzed again, this time from his pocket. Ruby was gazing out the window, her eyes soft and far-off, and since she didn't need his immediate attention, he pulled his phone out of his pocket. A second message from Dad.

He hadn't got the phone unlocked by the time Lena was exiting her exam room.

To his surprise, it was a mother and son who exited the room. He'd seen the boy of about twelve last week at the clinic.

"Hello," Lena said. "Let me clean up the exam room and I'll be ready for you," she told Ruby.

The mother and son didn't look at Todd as they walked past him, both averting their faces.

The white bandage on the boy's arm was fresh.

And Todd's temper sparked.

He didn't follow the mother and son outside, but he did follow Lena into her exam room. The bed had already been stripped, he guessed from before her recent patient.

"Do you have a medical degree I don't know about?" he asked.

She glanced up at him from the opposite side of the bed, where she flipped a corner of the sheet over. "What?"

"Are you seeing my patients?" he demanded.

"Of course not." But a flush stole into her cheeks. She knew what he was referring to. "Andrea is my friend and she asked me to look at Nick's arm. They're treating him at home."

"With burdock and some ointment I've never heard of before. Against my advice." Andrea had told him about the home remedy she intended to use at the appointment.

She shook her head as she tucked in the corner of the fitted sheet. The other side slipped off, probably because her movements had become agitated.

He wasn't a monster. He went and grabbed the opposite corner, earning a reluctant appreciative look from her.

"The boy's burn was third-degree. It covered almost all of his forearm. He needs a skin graft," Todd said. "The procedure won't take long. If it's an issue of cost—"

"It isn't," she said. "Andrea and her husband trust *Gott* to heal him."

It was Todd's turn to shake his head. "That burdock remedy isn't proven."

"Many Amish families use burdock to treat burns."

The night after Andrea had refused his referral to a Columbus plastic surgeon, he'd spent three hours squinting at his laptop screen, poring over medical papers. There'd been some research done on burdock. It did have antimicrobial properties. But *if* it worked—and in many cases, it didn't—the recovery was much longer than a simple skin graft.

He felt a stress headache building behind his right eye. He snapped the sheet into place and straightened.

So did she. Her chin was tilted at a stubborn angle. Her eyes flashed.

And he felt a peculiar twist in his stomach. She was *pretty*.

"Knock knock." Ruby stood at the doorway. "If you're finished arguing, could I come in?"

Lena smiled, but it wasn't like the open

smiles she'd given out on that first day when they'd worked in the clinic together. There was a tightness around her lips. "We weren't arguing."

Ruby glanced between them, her eyes narrowing slightly. "I'd like to see Lena alone, if that's all right."

Her words made his stomach tighten into a ball. He worked to show no expression.

His own sister-in-law didn't want him to consult at her prenatal appointment?

"Of course it's fine," he said calmly.

But he felt anything but calm.

It wasn't fine.

Lena didn't believe in lying, but she knew that Todd wasn't telling the entire truth.

All she'd done was change Nick's bandage. Should she have sent him and Andrea to the clinic?

He left the room and closed the door behind him.

And she was so discombobulated from the confrontation that she forgot to take Ruby's vitals until Ruby gently reminded her.

Her friend was kind enough not to remark on Lena's flustered state.

"Todd can be quite…"

"Intimidating?" Lena finished the statement

when Ruby trailed off. She wrapped the blood pressure cuff around Ruby's arm.

"Hmm. It's not that exactly. Something about his confidence, though."

Lena was glad for the excuse not to answer as she plugged in the stethoscope to her ears and began to squeeze air into the cuff.

It was his presence, she decided as she wrote Ruby's vitals on her paper patient record. When he entered a room, a person took notice. He was used to commanding his surroundings. She'd noticed it during the day she'd helped at the clinic.

It wasn't exactly a quality that would endear him to the community.

And somehow it always made her stomach flip.

She finished Ruby's exam but when she ushered her friend into the waiting area, Todd was nowhere to be seen. She heard noises from the kitchen and went that direction.

He was there, standing near the counter. He looked completely out of place in his *Englisher* clothes, a crisp white shirt and gray slacks, with his head down and eyes on his phone in his hand.

She must've made some noise, because he glanced up. He slipped his phone into his pocket.

"I hope you don't mind," he said. "I helped myself to some coffee." He lifted the mug she hadn't noticed on the counter in a salute before he lifted it to his lips.

"He skipped lunch," Ruby murmured from behind her.

"Of course I don't mind." She moved into the room, gesturing to the round table and chairs in the breakfast nook that looked out on her small garden and back yard. "Doc Bradshaw always made himself at home, and you should, too."

Something unreadable was in Todd's expression as she came near. Her face heated and she dropped her eyes to the floor.

"Ruby was my last appointment for the day." She shooed him toward the table.

Ruby joined Todd at the table as Lena puttered around the kitchen, quickly plating some leftover fried chicken and mashed potatoes that she'd enjoyed for supper yesterday.

"You don't have to feed me," Todd protested when she set the plate on the table in front of him.

She'd forgotten that she'd left out some of *Aendi* Carol's business records. She'd been poring over them this morning and the documents were spread across the table. Lena swept them into a pile, frowning down at them. She knew the process of birthing a baby inside and out, but reading over the business registration documents was like reading early German, a language she couldn't hope to muddle through.

She forced herself to focus. She hadn't answered Todd's statement that she wasn't required to feed him.

"The Bible says we are to love our neighbor," she said. "I suppose that includes feeding him when he is hungry."

Todd stared at the food while Ruby looked on, her mouth twitching in a smile.

"Thank you," he said finally. "I'm not sure I deserve your kindness after I barked at you in your exam room."

He bit into the chicken, a low groan showing his pleasure at the taste. She stifled a smile, even as Ruby giggled.

She waited until he'd eaten several bites before she spoke again. "You're forgiven. I apologize for snapping at you." Her gaze fell to the stack of papers on the counter. It had been almost a week and she was no closer to solving what she hoped was only a paperwork problem.

Her *mamm* had asked for help with some spring cleaning, a task that had taken most of two days. Lena had balked under the delay, but she also hadn't been able to refuse her mother.

After this morning had left her head swimming from reading the business registration papers, she'd decided she should go to the state department of health office in person. Someone there could tell her how to put together the packet of forms that seemed so difficult.

She blinked those thoughts away. Todd was here, and it was a chance to make nice.

Todd's fork clanked against his nearly empty plate when he laid it down. "What am I doing wrong?" he asked.

She felt her brows wrinkle as confusion set in at his words.

"Foot traffic at the clinic has dwindled to almost nothing. I came here to help, but how can I, if no one comes to the clinic? My own sister-in-law doesn't want to see me."

There was an undercurrent of hurt in his voice, and Ruby looked surprised. "It isn't that," she said. "It is a bit awkward to visit my husband's *bruder* as a doctor. I would feel the same awkwardness if you were one of my own *bruders*."

Todd looked surprised, as if he hadn't even considered that. "Really?"

"*Ja.*"

He glanced at Lena with those sharp, intelligent eyes. "Then why is the clinic empty? Why are my patients coming to you? Or staying away completely?"

"You really want to know?" she asked.

"Yes. I took feedback all the time during my residency. I need to know."

He glanced at his watch. She'd seen it on his wrist as they'd worked together. It was almost as sophisticated as his phone. Had it buzzed or lit up? His glance seemed almost habitual, as if he couldn't help himself.

"When I observed you seeing patients, you had your nose buried in your computer."

His eyes flashed with surprise. He'd told her to be honest with him, but maybe he hadn't expected her frankness. She could see from his expression that he wanted to argue, but he held his tongue.

So she went on, "You were more focused on the visit than the person. You rushed through each one."

His eyes glittered. "I suppose Doc Bradshaw was the kind of doctor that spent an hour with each patient? Talking about the weather and their grandchildren and everything in between?"

He made it sound like a punishment.

"Doc Bradshaw did like to take his time," Ruby said.

Todd pushed up from the table. "Maybe he spent time with his patients, but he certainly didn't keep up with his record keeping. His patient files are a mess."

And it was obvious from his tone that Todd found that unacceptable.

"He had a good memory," Ruby said.

Todd scowled. "Memories can fail. And what am I supposed to do—what about the doctor who ends up replacing him?" he asked. "He or she will have to re-create all the records that should've been there in the first place."

He must've seen the frown she couldn't hide. "What?"

She propped her hands on her hips. "You're still talking about *records*. About *medical histories*. Doc Bradshaw cared about the *people*."

He shook his head. He clearly didn't understand what she meant.

"You were quick to dismiss our home remedies," she said. "But Doc Bradshaw knew about them. And appreciated them. They are a part of our lives that have been handed down from generation to generation."

"But—"

"If you want patients to trust you, to come to the clinic, you might start by getting to know them."

She couldn't keep the tart tone from her voice. "You may even find you like one or two of us."

Chapter Five

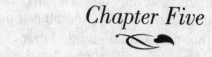

After a fruitless hour inside, Lena stood on the steps in front of the department of health building, clutching the folder of half-finished paperwork she'd brought with her.

She hadn't been able to meet with anyone who could help her, but she had determined that the letter had come from a Mr. Huffman's office.

Mr. Huffman was the director of the health department. He hadn't been in the office today. She'd hoped to find someone to help her figure out what paperwork was missing or what she needed to file, but she'd been sent from one desk to another. Both women had been busy and curt with her and they'd told her she could find the information she needed online. *Online*. As if she was familiar with the internet.

They'd taken one look at her simple home-made dress and dismissed her.

She could have done more good back at home. There were at least two expecting mothers who could deliver in the next week or two. She'd visited both of them yesterday and felt fairly certain she could take this trip to Columbus today without risk that they would go into labor.

She had ridden to the city with a local *Englisher* couple who had planned to visit family, Geoff and Audrey. She hadn't been sure how long her task would take—she couldn't have known she would fail so spectacularly so quickly. On the drive in, she had seen a public park several blocks down and across the street. She would wait there for a bit and then find a phone to call Geoff and find out whether they were ready to head back to Hickory Hollow.

She had her arms wrapped around the folder, pressed against her middle as she waited at the crosswalk, then crossed on green.

A fancy red car that reminded her of Todd passed by.

Todd.

He'd seemed nonplussed two days ago when she'd told him that he only saw cases, not people. Maybe she shouldn't have been so blunt. But he'd asked…

There was little traffic, and as she watched, the red car made a U-turn right there in the street.

And then rolled to a stop at the curb next to her. The window rolled down to reveal Todd in the driver's seat.

"Hey, there." When he smiled like that, her stomach did a little shimmy. "What are you doing here?"

"I had some business to attend to." She nodded at the administration building. "What are you doing here?"

"My parents have been checking my mail and they let me know a package I'd been waiting for arrived. Do you—you're not walking all the way back to Hickory Hollow, are you?"

She laughed a little and shook her head. "I have a ride, but I got done a bit earlier than I thought I would. It's a nice morning. I'll wait in the park." Though it was a bit more brisk than she'd thought it would be, out in the breeze.

He glanced in the mirror above his windshield. There was still no traffic behind him. "I'm heading back now. I would be happy to give you a ride."

The breeze loosened strands of her hair and blew them across one cheek. The chill down her back made the decision for her. "That would be nice."

He must've pressed a button from inside the car, because the passenger door opened.

She slipped inside, and he waited for her to buckle her seat belt before he slipped into what little traffic there was.

"Thank you." She shivered and he pressed something on the screen between them. She'd never seen such a high-tech car.

"Heated seats," he said. "We'll warm you right up." He quirked one eyebrow, as if he expected her to be impressed.

"It's nice. Usually in the winter, I heat a brick for my feet when I ride in the buggy."

"Takes longer," he commented.

She glanced out the window at the passing city blocks. "Not everything has to be instant. Have you ever wondered if your life is passing too quickly?"

He cut a glance at her while he braked for a stoplight. "No. I've never thought of it like that." Another glance. "Although what did you say about my bedside manner? I rushed each patient in and out?"

It wasn't quite how she'd phrased it, but she felt a wash of chagrin anyway. "I shouldn't have been so hard on you."

"I asked you for your honest opinion. And I appreciated your honesty, even if it was difficult to hear."

His complimentary words made her blush even hotter. She looked down at her lap. "Would you mind if I borrowed your phone to let my ride know I'm already heading home?"

"Sure."

But he didn't hand her the device. He slowed down and pulled into a parking lot. A coffee shop.

He tapped the phone screen a few times and then handed it to her to type in the number. It only took a matter of moments to let Geoff know she'd found another ride. She handed the phone back to Todd.

He motioned to the coffee shop outside the window. "Let's go in. Do you want a cup of coffee?"

"Oh, that's all right."

He quirked that eyebrow at her again. "Didn't you just tell me to stop rushing? Do you have somewhere to be?"

"Well, no—"

"Good." He was already getting out of the car. There was no stopping him.

She sighed and got out, too, leaving her folder behind.

Inside, the strong aroma of coffee beans and

sweet baked goods filtered through the air. College-aged young people sat at the small round tables. A woman typed on her laptop. Two older men argued over some papers laid out on another table.

The barista greeted them warmly. The menu was like a foreign language, and when Todd looked to her for her order, she simply said, "I'll just have whatever you're having."

When she reached into her pocket for some of the spare cash she'd brought, he waved her off. "My treat."

She joined him at one of the small tables. She caught a sideways glance from one of the maybe-college students.

"Does it bother you?" Todd asked, voice low. He nodded to the student. He must've noticed, too.

She shook her head. "I am comfortable with who I am. The difference just is more noticeable somewhere like here."

His eyes were warm. "I like that about you."

The barista brought their coffees in tall paper cups with plastic lids. She took a sip, the coffee flavored with caramel and lightened with cream. "It's good. Thank you."

He held one hand wrapped around his cup on the table. "Tell me about yourself."

Heat rose in her cheeks again. "When I said for you to get to know the people from our community, I didn't mean me."

"Why not? We're going to be working together, aren't we? And I can't seem to stop thinking about what you said."

His words stumped her momentarily and she was trying to figure out a way to deflect when he went on, "You said Doc Bradshaw knew everybody. I'm guessing that included you. So I'll need to get to know you, too." He sipped his coffee. "We can start with something easy. What're you doing in Columbus today?"

She frowned. "That isn't easy. I received a letter from the department of health that stated the birthing center is out of compliance. I can't find any notes among my *aendi's*—my aunt's—paperwork. I thought I could speak to someone in the director's office, but it seemed as if I only got the runaround."

He looked thoughtful. "Is it possible she never filed as a hospital?"

"I don't know. She started the birthing center thirty years ago. I'm sure it was only word of mouth back then, when a new mother wanted to have a baby at Carol's home. I don't know if she would've even thought that she needed to register."

His head dipped toward the table. Fingers of his opposite hand tapped on his knee. "Have you wondered if it wouldn't be easier to shut down the center? Send all the women to the hospital instead?"

Todd knew he'd said the wrong thing when the open expression vanished from Lena's face. She frowned fiercely at her coffee. She'd barely drunk any of it.

"I'm not sure the women would go to the hospital," she said finally. "If there wasn't a birthing center, I think many of them would choose to have their babies at home."

A sense of panic stole into his chest as he remembered Elise Tanner on a gurney, blood everywhere. She'd been admitted to the ER through the ambulance bay and he'd jumped in from the moment she'd come through the doorway. He'd been a first year resident and his attending had been at his elbow the entire time, but in the end, the work they'd done to try and save her hadn't been enough.

He hadn't thought about Elise in a long time.

He only remembered her name because of how devastated he'd been. In the ER, he saw numerous patients every day, their names forgotten. Usually they were discharged before his next shift.

"Todd?"

His tight grip on the coffee cup had pushed the liquid upward, and he'd sloshed coffee out of the small hole in the lid. It was a wonder it hadn't burst in his shaking hand.

"Sorry." He cleared his throat, pushed the memories away. "Tell me something else about you."

"Like what?" She still had her walls up, and he badly needed the distraction of conversation right now.

"How many siblings do you have?" He pulled the question from thin air.

"Four sisters. Two older and two younger. I have six nieces and nephews."

Her voice held clear affection for them.

"Have you ever wanted kids?" he asked. "Sorry—that was impertinent. Again."

It didn't stop him from wanting to know, especially when her eyes flashed to his and quickly away.

"Do you have brothers or sisters? Other than David?"

Of course, she knew about David. It had been a major stir in the community, from what he'd gathered talking with his brother.

"I have one younger brother. Henry. He's a general contractor. He builds and remodels houses."

"Are you close?"

That was difficult to answer. He sipped his coffee first. "We used to be. Med school was a big commitment and we've grown apart."

Henry had been even more distant since Todd had made the discovery that their long-lost brother lived ninety minutes from home.

"What's one of your favorite memories with him?"

He looked at her as she sipped her coffee. The adorable tilt at the end of her nose, the way her eyes hinted that she was on the cusp of smiling.

When they'd come inside, he'd only been able to think about how she looked so different from everyone else inside the shop. It was her dress and that prayer *kapp*.

But now he didn't see anyone else. And he didn't want to look away.

"When I was a freshman in college, he wanted to try out for the high school basketball team—and he was pretty awful. We spent every day of my Christmas break from university on my parents' driveway, where they had a basketball hoop. He didn't get much better, but we laughed so much…"

He glanced out the window into the bright morning sunlight but didn't really see the traffic outside. He hadn't thought about that time with Henry in forever.

Was it his fault they'd grown apart? Between med school and studying and then his grueling residency, there were never enough hours in the day.

"It sounds like you should find a basketball hoop and play with your brother again." Lena's soft words shook him out of his thoughts. "Now I'm the one being impertinent."

She was staring down at the table when he glanced back at the table and at her.

"You're probably right. I should text him."

She wrinkled her nose before she drank from her coffee again.

"What?" he asked. "You don't like my phone? Texting?"

She shook her head. "I didn't say anything."

"You made a face."

Her eyes flashed.

He liked teasing her.

She ducked her head again. "It just seems so…impersonal. Why don't you see him?"

"Because I'm busy." The words rang a little hollow, though.

"Not too busy to come to the city today," she said.

He'd never given it much thought, but he'd always assumed Amish women were meek and passive.

Lena wasn't afraid to challenge him.

"Henry has a job, too," he said. "But you're right. We should get together. There's a big family reunion coming up, on my father's side. I'll see him then and make sure to tell him I'd like to get together more often."

Although he probably wouldn't have time once he started his new job in the Lakeview Barrett Hospital ER. Even bearing Grandfather's name, he was still the new guy. He'd get the worst shifts, sometimes be expected to work doubles. He wasn't done proving himself, just because his residency was over.

Thinking about his job reminded him that his time in Hickory Hollow was short. His coffee was empty, so he leaned one forearm on the table.

"How can I get to know your people?" he asked. "I've been thinking a lot about what you said. But if no one walks through the clinic door, how am I supposed to accomplish it?"

She blinked at him for a moment, her gaze on his face. She shook herself out of a daze and looked down to where she was fingering her coffee cup. "How well have you gotten to know the Schrock family?"

He grimaced.

And she noticed. "They haven't offered to share meals with you?"

"They have," he admitted. "I put them off. I didn't want to be a burden."

"They wouldn't have offered hospitality unless they meant it."

It was his turn to wrinkle his nose. "Fine."

"Would David let you tag along with him one day? You'd meet some folks and see what he does."

He'd never thought of it, but it was a great idea. When he told her so, Lena turned her face.

And then she sat up straight, as if startled. "I know just the thing. Are you finished? We can go now."

Chapter Six

"What is this?"

Lena couldn't help but smile at Todd's perplexed look. He stopped the car on the gravel country road well back from the house—or what would become the house.

Right now it was a skeleton, the two-by-fours that would become walls exposed to the noontime sun.

Amish buggies lined the road and the driveway. Men worked on the house while children helped or ran around the surrounding large yard. Women were gathered in groups, chatting or setting out food on long tables set up out of the way of the builders.

"It looks like the whole town is here." He sounded impressed.

Or maybe that was just her hope. She'd felt

something stir inside her, sitting in that coffee shop across from him. He'd seemed…lonely. Not only when he'd spoken about his brother, but she'd sensed it, too, when he'd asked her how to reach her people.

"It's a house raising," she told him now. "Samuel and Elizabeth are getting married in a month. This is her father's property, and they'll need a place of their own to start their new family."

"I didn't think people did things like this anymore."

"House raisings don't happen often, but we help each other when needed."

He stared out the windshield, one hand resting on top of the steering wheel.

"Let's go," she suggested.

He glanced at her askance. "You mean, go help?"

"Yes." She laughed a little. "You said your brother is a builder, didn't you?"

"But I'm not," he protested.

"That's all right. Maybe you can hold a tape measure or something."

He pulled a face at her. When they got out of the car, she looked over the top of the vehicle at him.

"I dare you to leave your phone in the car."

He cocked one eyebrow.

"Join in without any distractions. You might be surprised what happens."

He closed his car door. "I can't leave it behind—it's my key for the car. But I'll leave it in my pocket. Promise."

They walked side by side, approaching some of the women first, including Lena's cousin Terri and her two toddler boys.

"Lena! Lena!" The boys chanted. The older of the two, Randy, darted toward her.

She swept him into her arms "Hello, son of Jacob. Are you helping your *mamm* today?"

He nodded, sticking a thumb in his mouth when he realized Todd was standing next to her.

She introduced them and Todd was full of warm smiles.

"How old are you, young man?" Todd asked the little boy.

Randy held up three fingers. His other hand was still in his mouth.

"Three? That's big."

Randy popped his hand out of his mouth. "I can drive a cart with my dog Brownie. An' my brovver Mikey is too wittle to do it. Only I can."

"Wow. That's impressive."

"Randy and Mikey were both born at the center," Lena murmured.

"Cousin Lena is *goot* at her job," Terri added.

"*Onkle* Todd!" a high voice exclaimed just before Mindy ran up to them. Ruby was on her heels, and Maggie was on her mother's hip. Ruby looked a little peaked.

Todd picked up Mindy and tweaked her nose. "Hey, munchkin."

"You're a munchkin," she said.

"I am?" He took one look at Ruby and put Mindy down. "You okay? Do you need to sit down?"

"I'm fine. I'll be better once we eat."

One of her friends nearby went in search of some crackers.

"I'm surprised to see you," Ruby said.

"Lena brought me."

Lena felt Ruby's glance—and more from the other women nearby—like a scorching touch. It hadn't been *like that*. She hadn't come *with* Todd. They weren't together.

She'd heard what he hadn't said in the coffee shop earlier. He missed the connection he'd once had with his younger brother. He wanted connection with David, wanted to know his temporary neighbors.

"What better way to get to know the community than today?" she murmured.

Thankfully, Ruby's attention shifted to Todd.

"David is there." She pointed to the back corner of what was beginning to look like a house. "He would love to see you, to have you work next to him today."

"Ah. All right." There'd only been a small hesitation before Todd sent her one more glance, then strode off toward his brother.

He looked so different in his jeans and knitted shirt. As out of place as Lena must've been, sitting in that *Englisher* coffee shop.

"Are you making friends, then?" Ruby asked warmly.

She put Randy down when he began to wiggle. He ran off to join a gaggle of older boys.

"Todd saw me in the city and was kind enough to offer a ride home. He mentioned that patients hadn't been coming in to the clinic as frequently as before and that he wanted to get to know our community better."

She wasn't sure why, but she didn't mention the coffee shop. She wasn't breaking any rules having a simple cup of coffee with an *Englisher*. It hadn't been a date. There was nothing like that between her and Todd.

Or her and anyone.

And yet…there was a part of her that wanted to keep those moments to herself.

Ruby swayed a little with Maggie in her

arms. The little one laid her head on her mother's shoulder. "David will be happy his brother is here. I don't think he has seen Todd as much as he'd hoped when he invited him to come here and help with the clinic."

Was Todd holding back? If so, why?

A cry from a small voice rang out, and moments later, another boy escorted Randy back to his mother, who still stood near Lena.

"He got stung. I think it was a bee."

Randy was sobbing as his mother handed off Mikey and crouched down to his level.

Lena saw the tender way her hand moved over his hair. "Where does it hurt?" Terri asked.

Lena had to look away when her stomach pinched.

And then the sound of Randy's sobs changed. What had been normal cries was suddenly a struggle for him to draw breath.

"Lena!" Terri cried.

She took one step closer and saw his wide, panicked eyes amid his flushed and mottled face. His skin had whitened around his mouth.

"Someone get Doctor Todd," she ordered.

Footsteps faded away from behind her, voices rang out, but she kept her focus on Randy.

"Lay him down," she told Terri. "Where was he stung?"

She knelt next to him, ready to move the moment Todd got close.

His left arm was covered in hives, already swollen and red.

He gasped for breath. His chest moving in jerky movements that didn't seem to help.

Lena put her fingers to his wrist to take his pulse. It was reedy and thin.

Terri was looking at Lena expectantly, but she wasn't a doctor. Most births followed a predictable rhythm. When they didn't, Doc Bradshaw had always been there to help. Or she'd sent her patient on to the hospital.

She didn't know how to help Randy. But she knew it was bad.

"What happened?"

Todd was there, at her elbow. And then kneeling across from her.

He was all business, his eyes flicking over the boy before he knelt in the dirt and grass, heedless of his clothes.

For the first time, she was grateful for his focus.

"Stephen brought him over. He said Randy was stung by a bee."

Terri. That was little Randy's mother.

"His pulse is weak," Lena murmured.

That fit the symptoms Todd could see. He lifted the boy's eyelids to look at his pupils.

His training kicked in, not only the textbook knowledge he'd worked so hard to obtain, but memories of the patients he'd treated in the ER under his attending physician.

"He's in anaphylactic shock."

Terri gasped.

Lena didn't seem surprised.

Todd had only dealt with patients like this in the hospital, where there was oxygen and nurses and medication.

"He needs epinephrine." The drug would stop the reaction long enough for them to make it to a hospital. "Do you have an EpiPen?"

Terri shook her head. Someone must've gotten Randy's father, because a man in Amish garb with a short black beard stood beside her now, looking worried.

"Nothing like this has ever happened before," the man said.

Everything at the building site had stopped. No hammers rang out. No voices spoke.

Everyone was watching Todd.

"He's having an allergic reaction to the bee sting," he called out to the onlookers. "He's going into shock. Does anyone have an EpiPen?"

It was a long shot to ask, and he wasn't surprised when no one answered in the affirmative.

Randy's lips were turning blue. They were running out of time.

His brain scrambled for a solution that would save this boy's life. No EpiPen.

He carried a basic kit in his trunk, but no medications.

The clinic.

"The clinic has a STAT kit," he said.

Doc Bradshaw had showed it to him briefly during that first day. And since Todd hadn't had any patients after noon two days ago, he'd gone through each medication inside the emergency kit and checked that they weren't expired.

"We need to get him to the clinic," he explained.

The boy's father was already lifting Randy into his arms.

"Lena, come with us," Terri gasped.

Todd didn't have time to argue. "My car will be faster than a buggy."

The five of them, with Randy in his father's arms, set out at a run.

Todd unlocked his phone and passed it to Lena as they reached the car. "Call 911. Ask them to send an ambulance to the clinic."

He helped Terri and her husband into the

back seat. He heard Lena speaking into the phone, rattling off the address for the clinic.

He slipped into the driver's seat and quickly reversed so he could drive to the clinic.

Randy's reedy breaths rattled through the car.

Todd wished someone else could be driving so he could keep an eye on the boy. But that wasn't reality. No one at that work site could drive.

Helpless anger boiled through him that there wasn't an emergency room nearby, but he couldn't focus on that right now.

It took less than five minutes to reach the clinic, but it felt like a lifetime.

"Can you help them bring him into exam one?" he asked Lena.

She nodded.

"I'll get the emergency kit."

It was in the supply closet, where he'd seen it last. A blast of relief hit him.

It only took a moment to grab the EpiPen. He grabbed the pediatric version, then hustled into the exam room.

"He stopped breathing!" Terri cried out.

Lena stood next to where the boy lay on the exam table. Terri's husband pulled her out of the way as Todd approached.

He didn't hesitate before clicking the release and administering the EpiPen.

It took less than a second for Randy to take a rattling breath. Then another one, slightly more even.

"Can you take his blood pressure?" Todd asked Lena.

She was already reaching for the cuff as Todd turned to the counter where he pulled a stethoscope and pulse oximeter from the drawer.

A sob escaped Terri. Her husband said something to her that Todd couldn't make out.

Randy's eyes were open and he was wriggling on the table when Todd stood beside it.

"It's too tight!" Randy protested to Lena.

"Lie still," Todd said gently. "You'll be driving your cart in no time, but we need to check you over for now." He clipped the pulse ox to the boy's finger even as he slipped his stethoscope on and leaned in to listen to Randy's breathing.

The swelling in his airways had decreased considerably.

Todd met Lena's gaze as she gently disengaged the cuff from Randy's arm.

She nodded. She didn't attempt to tell him the BP number while he listened to Randy's breathing, but her nod was reassuring.

They'd done it. They had kept Randy alive.

A euphoric feeling, the same one he felt after a success in the ER, came over him, and he found himself grinning at her.

Her eyes searched his face. She smiled back.

He pulled the stethoscope from his ears. She rattled off Randy's blood pressure and Todd filed it away mentally.

Sirens wailed, getting closer.

Todd waved the couple over.

"He's going to be okay," Lena said to her cousin.

"You'll need to take him to the nearest hospital for monitoring overnight," Todd said.

The sirens were getting louder.

"But why?" Terri asked. "He looks much better."

Randy had regained the color in his face and was sitting up, playing with the pulse ox.

"The epinephrine stopped the reaction for now, but his body could still react to the bee sting. A hospital is equipped to help him if that happens."

Todd continued explaining why it was necessary—what could happen if Randy went into shock again or how he might even have a rare, unexpected reaction to the epinephrine. Finally, they understood.

He followed them out to meet the ambulance while Lena stayed behind. The EMTs listened to his quick, concise explanation and Randy's vitals as the boy was loaded into the ambulance.

And then the ambulance drove off, with Randy and his parents inside.

The crucial moments were over. Todd's adrenaline began to fade as he watched the bulky automobile drive away.

Inside the clinic, there was movement in the exam room.

Lena was wiping down the table and disposing of the medication in the sharps bin.

"You didn't have to do that," he said in surprise. "Clean up."

"I know." But she went on to wipe down the counter anyway.

He went to his office and made a note that the STAT kit would need to be replenished. He would call the hospital later to check on Randy. He didn't remember the family's last name and went to ask Lena.

She was spreading a new paper sheet over the exam table and soft afternoon light filtered in through the blinds at the window.

He was caught anew by her beauty. She had a generous heart, cleaning up when she didn't have to. She'd been calm in a frightening situation and almost seemed to read his mind in the office as they'd worked together.

She glanced up and caught him staring.

He cleared his throat.

"I am thanking *Gott* for you," she said with a gentle smile. "If you hadn't been there..."

A brush of the anger he'd buried earlier returned, making him frown. "What would the family have done if there'd been no EpiPen? It's dangerous not to have the necessary medical care out here."

She looked surprised at his question. "But we did have what we needed. We had you."

Chapter Seven

Lena was shocked to see Todd sitting next to David in house church that Sunday morning.

She sat with the women on wooden benches along one side of the John Miller family's large basement. The men sat along the opposite side, and there was Todd, sitting next to his brother. He wore a white dress shirt and dark pants, and might've passed for Amish if he'd added suspenders. And if he had a beard. In their community, most men his age had been married for years. Most had small children.

David was two years younger than Todd, and his third child was on the way.

Thinking about Todd being married made her stomach twist and she forced herself to focus on the singing and then the message delivered by the bishop.

She sat in her usual place next to *Aendi* Kate. On her other side, her younger sister Julie, held her infant daughter Claire.

When Bishop Bontrager stood to deliver his sermon, Julie groaned a little under her breath. She leaned her shoulder into Lena's, "Can you take her?"

Lena was happy to hold the wriggling ten-month-old.

She glanced at Julie, who was breathing deeply through her nose. She looked a little green.

Oh.

Lena's mind leaped ahead. Julie might be pregnant again.

Her heart pinched, but she pushed that feeling aside as she looked down into Claire's face.

Claire's big, blue eyes focused on Lena. She smiled a drooly smile as she pushed one tiny fist into her mouth.

Lena did her best to entertain the baby while also not distracting the worshippers around her.

By the end of the bishop's sermon, Claire was fast asleep in her arms.

"I'll take her upstairs for you," Lena said to her sister.

Julie nodded, still looking a bit green.

Today, the church members would eat a meal together upstairs in the Millers' home. Children darted through the crowd toward the stairs to the first floor.

The women headed upstairs to help Susan Miller lay out the lunch that was already prepared.

The men carried up the benches for additional places to sit.

Lena was careful not to jostle Claire as she moved through the crowd toward the stairs. She nodded hellos to several people.

"Good morning." Todd's voice was low and close.

She glanced over her shoulder to find him there. Maggie was in his arms.

Lena turned to face him better. "Hello." She was still moving at a slow shuffle toward the stairs, but he joined her.

"Baby!" Maggie squealed, pointing at Claire.

"Shh," Todd shushed her. "That's right. Look, she's sleeping."

Maggie twisted so she was looking over Todd's shoulder. He soothed her with his palm on her back.

His eyes met Lena's. "Hi."

A strange shyness descended over her. She felt almost...bashful. "Hi."

"Is that little one related to you?" he asked when the silence went on a beat too long.

She shuffled forward a step. "My niece. Claire."

"I saw you playing with her earlier."

He was watching her during the sermon? Imagining it sent little prickles of awareness dancing across her skin.

"I am surprised to see you here," she admitted.

"David invited me."

She'd guessed as much. She tilted her head to see his face better. "What did you think of our service?"

"It was…long." He grinned at her and she couldn't help shaking her head at his boyish, teasing answer.

"I'm sure you attend a church with an efficient, twenty-minute service back home." She didn't know where the teasing words came from.

He laughed and the sound sent a tiny flock of butterflies fluttering in her stomach.

She forced herself to look away. Her gaze met *Aendi* Kate's curious one, and she remembered where she was. Surrounded by family and friends. All of whom would see her talking with Todd.

She asked more seriously, "What is your church like at home? Do you have one?"

He nodded. "We have a praise band and a coffee shop, and it *is* a lot different than this gathering. But your bishop reminds me of my pastor. Both men deliver sermons that make me think, long after the service is over."

They gained the stairs. It was almost a relief to be in a room with windows that let in sunlight. Lena moved out of the flow of traffic and farther into the living room. She found an empty corner and resolved to stay out of the way.

Todd had followed her and stood nearby. Maggie was chattering to him about something out the window.

Claire made a soft noise and stretched in her sleep. Lena swayed side to side and the gentle movement settled the babe, who drifted off again.

Todd's gaze landed on Lena and Claire. "You're good with her."

"I hold a lot of babies when their mothers are at the center."

He tipped his head, considering her. "It's more than that, I think. You never did tell me why you don't have a family of your own."

Her heartbeat sped up. "You said it was an impertinent question."

"I did." Something moved behind his eyes. "But that doesn't mean I don't want to know."

His intent look sent a blush to her cheeks. She looked down at Claire's sleeping face. "Maybe I'm not the marrying kind."

He chuckled, and it startled her so she looked up at him.

His eyes searched her face and his mirth faded. "You're not serious."

Her chin jutted.

And she was saved from saying anything else by Ruby and David's approach. Mindy was between them.

"Oh, Lena! Hello." Ruby's warm greeting was a perfect interruption. "I think they are about to start serving."

"I'm hungry!" Mindy whined.

"Hungry!" Maggie punctuated her word with a little fist pounding on Todd's shoulder.

"You should join us," Ruby said.

The disconcerting moment with Todd made her want to say no. She looked around the crowded room. It was full of people talking in clusters, but no one from her family was in sight.

Mindy tugged on her skirt. "Please, Lena!"

The weight of Todd's stare lay upon her shoulders even as she kept her focus on the little girl.

"How can I say no to you?" she teased Mindy.

Claire would wake from her nap soon enough. She'd need her mother then, so Lena would have a way to escape, if she needed it.

Todd found himself seated at a long table with Mindy at one elbow and David on her other side, with Maggie on his knee. He had a plate full of roast and vegetables and a fluffy sweet roll in front of him. The murmur of many conversations showed how full the room was, but somehow their little cluster seemed to be in its own world.

Lena and Ruby sat across from Todd and David. Lena still held the sleeping baby.

There was something about her this morning. He couldn't keep himself from staring.

He couldn't fathom that he'd thought she was plain when they'd first met. The last time they'd been together, he'd noticed just how beautiful she was.

And how he couldn't seem to *keep* from noticing.

It didn't have to mean anything. He could appreciate a woman's beauty without pursuing her.

And there was no way he could expect anything more than friendship from Lena. They lived in different worlds.

He didn't even know if she was allowed to date an *Englisher* like him.

Nothing could come of it.

And yet…he still couldn't help himself from noticing the way her lashes made dark fans against her cheeks when she dipped her head to take a bite. Ruby said something to her, and she smiled, a quick flash of white teeth.

A response reverberated through him, even though she hadn't asked a question.

"Do you do this every week?" he asked David, needing a distraction. "It seems like a massive amount of work."

David smiled patiently. "We worship and eat together every other Sunday. It is a *goot* deal of work, but neighbors and families help each other. The family that hosts changes each time we're together, so no one family is overburdened."

Todd thought of the house raising. It had seemed like every Amish family in town had been present. He'd driven by the site yesterday and been astounded to see that the house appeared complete, with small flower bushes planted in the front garden and a clothesline strung in the yard.

When he wasn't thinking about Lena, he was

thinking about Hickory Hollow. It was so different from what he'd known his entire life.

"I was hoping Henry would make it today," David said. The offhand comment seemed innocent, but Todd knew David was hurt by Henry's standoffish ways.

"Me, too. I left him two voice mails." He'd called his brother after Lena had inspired him during their coffee shop conversation.

He tipped his head to include her in the conversation. "Maybe he finally returned my call, but I wouldn't know. I left my phone in the car."

A smile spread across her lips. "That must be terrible for you. How many times have you reached for it?"

"Too many," he admitted with a self-deprecating grin.

He hated to admit that she'd been right. He needed the phone at certain times. He had to be reachable at all times when he was on call—which wouldn't happen until he started his job at Lakeview.

But maybe he'd made too much of a habit of reaching for his phone. He'd read from a leather-bound Bible this morning. He hadn't checked his emails numerous times during the service. He'd been more able to focus on the words of the songs being sung and the message in the sermon.

Maybe it was the slower pace here, but he felt a bit of a call to slow down. "If he called, I wouldn't know it."

"Is it so bad to have to wait to speak to him?" Her question seemed genuine.

"No. I guess not." It just went against the grain. He was used to instant access.

"I admire your resilience." But her lip was twitching with a smile.

Todd couldn't help noticing the glance that passed between David and Ruby.

Lena seemed oblivious. "You'd better keep your phone on for the next few days," she said. "Jane Glick was in for a checkup yesterday, and I expect she'll be giving birth any day."

She seemed thrilled at the prospect, but a tug in Todd's gut set him on edge. He still didn't want a baby to be birthed at the center.

But it didn't seem like he would have much choice in the matter.

"Did you attend many births during your residency?" Ruby asked curiously.

"A handful. Most women have their babies in the obstetrics wing. Obstetricians are specialized doctors who spend most of their time delivering babies," he explained. "But sometimes the baby won't wait and is delivered in the ambulance or in the ER."

"What does ER stand for?" Mindy asked, tipping her head up to look at him.

"Emergency room. That's where I work."

She scrunched her nose. "You're a doctor at the clinic."

He tapped the top of her head. "Only for a few more weeks. My real job is waiting for me. I will set broken bones and help people who've been in accidents." He didn't go into details. That wouldn't be appropriate for someone Mindy's age.

"It sounds exciting," Ruby said when the conversation lulled. Mindy had gone back to shoveling corn into her mouth.

"I love it," he said. "Every day is different. I never know what kind of patients I will see that day. It's fast-paced. Sometimes I don't even have time to eat. I have to be on the top of my game."

And he loved it.

Lena had gone quiet, staring at her plate as she scooped up the last of her mashed potatoes.

"Well, we are glad you are here, even if it is only for five more weeks." David was smiling, but there was something tight in his expression.

"You should come for supper," Ruby said.

Todd couldn't catch Lena's eye and blinked into focus his sister-in-law.

"What night?"

"All of them," she said. "It sounds like you'll be too busy to visit when you start your new job. We want to see you as much as we can before you go."

He pushed his empty plate back. "It won't be that bad. I won't be able to set my schedule at first—new guy and all—but after a few years I'll have more tenure."

A few years. Lena was looking down at the baby in her arms, but he still saw her mouth move.

He didn't know why the sudden distance between them should make him so uncomfortable, but it did.

He was proud of his job, proud of the good he'd done during his residency and what he'd do in the future. His family's name was emblazoned on the hospital wall and he had a legacy to uphold.

Maybe Lena couldn't understand what it took, the expectations that were laid on him. Gramps held high hopes for Todd's career.

But he missed the admiration he'd seen in her eyes when he'd saved little Randy.

"Mrs. Smith asked off for the morning tomorrow," he said. "Do you think you could help out at the clinic for a few hours?"

He had planned to handle the patient load himself. More patients had trickled in after what the folks had witnessed with Randy at the work site, but it still wasn't busy enough that he couldn't handle things on his own.

"I'll have to see," she said, still not quite looking at him. "I need to make sure the center is prepared for Jane."

That wasn't good enough.

"Maybe I can help you with your paperwork problem," he said. It was a gamble, but it paid off when she looked up at him. "Unless you've already solved it?"

She shook her head, her eyes slightly narrowed. "I'll have to see," she repeated.

But he knew he'd won. Unless there was a mother giving birth, Lena would come to the clinic tomorrow.

Chapter Eight

Todd had the coffee on this time when the front door to the clinic opened and Lena let herself in.

She had a small bag over her arm, and when she glanced up to see him at the coffee machine, she froze for a moment.

"Good morning," he said.

She blinked and lowered her eyes. "Harold and Amos are—"

"Outside. I know." He held up a Styrofoam coffee cup. "How do you take your coffee?"

"Oh. Umm. A dab of milk."

A dab of milk. He stored the knowledge away, though he couldn't pinpoint why.

He balanced three coffee cups in both his hands and headed for the door. She remained standing there, looking a little flummoxed.

He smiled at her and shouldered the door open, careful not to spill the coffee. "Join us?"

She still looked bewildered, but set her bag just to the side of the door and followed him out onto the sidewalk in front of the clinic.

He handed cups of coffee to the two men who sat side by side on the wooden bench outside the clinic.

Harold smiled gratefully, while Amos regarded him with a hint of suspicion.

Todd ignored it. "Good morning, you two. I didn't know how you took your coffee, so I hope black is all right."

"Black is fine," Harold mumbled.

Todd turned to Lena, who hesitated with one hand still on the door. He pressed the coffee cup into her empty hand. "Good morning," he murmured. "Thanks for helping out today."

He heard her quick intake of breath, but before she could say anything, Amos asked, "You aren't having a cup with us?"

Todd stuck his hands in his pockets and rocked back on his heels. "I've already had mine."

Amos scoffed just before he sipped his coffee.

Todd took a moment to look around. None of the other businesses were open yet. The sun was up, but hadn't been for long. Soft light filtered through the mature trees growing at intervals on either side of the street. There was no traffic and it was quiet and peaceful.

Beautiful. Especially with Lena beside him.

He took a deep breath, inhaling her clean scent. She didn't use fragrances.

"How are your feet?" he asked conversationally.

When Amos only grunted, Todd wondered whether the man had come for a follow-up visit. Maybe he hadn't broken the ice enough yet.

"Have you been taking your medication?" he asked Harold.

"Every day," the man said. "My wife makes sure of it."

So maybe this was a social visit? How could Todd be sure?

"How many grandchildren do you have?" he aimed the question at both men.

Amos squinted at him. "Just how old do you think we are?"

No grandchildren? He remembered their ages—in their seventies, both of them—because of the charting he'd done after their first visit to the clinic. But he couldn't remember whether Lena had mentioned grandchildren or not. He'd rather thought most Amish couples had children early, and their children had children early...

He looked to Lena for help, but she was sipping her coffee, the Styrofoam mug blocking most of her face from view. Were her eyes dancing?

He felt his own eyes narrowing.

It was Harold who took pity on him. "Amos, quit giving the *buwe* a hard time." To Todd, he said, "Of course we have grandkids. Amos has fifteen and I've got nine."

"What is *buwe*?" He had an inkling, but he asked Lena anyway.

"It means boy." A smile came through in her voice.

Boy? Todd hadn't been called a kid since high school. Maybe before then. He'd always been the mature one in his group of friends.

"My youngest grandson is only a month older than little Randy," Harold said.

"We heard what you did at the Bontrager place," Amos said.

Was that meant to be praise? Amos had only said he heard about it. Not that he thought Todd had done a good job.

Amos kept his eyes on the cup he was twisting in his hands. "You ever do house calls?"

"I...don't know." He glanced to Lena for help but her gaze was on Amos. "Did Doc Bradshaw make house calls? Of course he did," he answered his own question before any of the trio could.

If it was an outdated practice, it was a safe guess that Bradshaw had probably done it.

"I suppose I could stop by this afternoon," he said.

Amos grunted again. Was that an approving grunt?

Harold looked slightly relieved and nodded at Todd.

A young mother holding a baby in her arms walked up the sidewalk in their direction.

"Is the clinic open?" she asked breathlessly.

One glance at the two men. Harold lifted his cup in a salute. Todd guessed they'd gotten what they came for?

"We can see you now," he said. The clinic wasn't set to open for another half hour, but maybe he was getting used to being in Hickory Hollow, because he didn't feel the irritation he had only a week ago.

He opened the door for the young mother and then motioned Lena to precede him.

"Will they be all right?" he asked, with another glance over his shoulder at the two men.

"Mm-hmm." She was already disposing of her empty coffee cup. To the young mother, she said, "I'll wash my hands and meet you in the first exam room, just there."

Lena had barely said two words to him this morning.

Something felt different. Off.

He wracked his brain as he slipped down the hall to retrieve his coat. Had he said something wrong yesterday during their lunch together? They'd talked about his future in the ER. He didn't think he'd said anything too graphic or disgusting.

In his office, his cell phone was where he'd left it on the desk. It was buzzing against the desktop with an incoming call.

Grandfather.

He picked it up out of habit.

"What's this I hear about you taking a sabbatical?"

He could hear the frown in the older man's voice.

"Good morning, Grandfather. I—"

"I had to hear it from Jamison. A board of directors member and not my own grandson?"

The muscles in Todd's face tightened. He hated disappointing Grandfather. This is what he got for keeping quiet and hoping for forgiveness after the fact.

"It's only for a few weeks," he said as calmly as he could muster. "Elliott was fine with moving my start date back."

"You are a Barrett," Grandfather said. "We don't shirk our commitments."

"That's not what I'm doing." He rolled his shoulders, attempting to lose some of the tension there. "David asked me to come to Hickory Hollow for a few weeks."

Grandfather went silent. Finding out that David was Mom and Dad's biological son and that he was alive and well had sent shock waves through the family. Grandfather might be driven and career-focused and a little meddlesome, but surely even he could understand why Todd had needed to come.

The silence stretched and Todd checked the phone to make sure he hadn't lost the connection.

"I pulled strings to get you this job," Grandfather said.

"I know. I'm grateful. And I'll be there on my new start date."

Grandfather harrumphed.

"I was just telling David how excited I am to be there."

But in the wake of Grandfather's frustration, some of Todd's excitement had waned.

There was movement in the hallway outside. "I have to go."

He rang off and tapped his phone on his

thigh, staring sightlessly at Bradshaw's big bookshelf. Grandfather had been angry.

But that wasn't unexpected.

Todd would smooth things over.

Grandfather was a strong patriarch in their family. He'd disowned Todd's cousin Tyler, who hadn't fallen in line with his demands.

But Todd could prove that coming to Hickory Hollow had been the right choice. Probably.

Lena spent the morning focusing on the patients and keeping her hands busy.

And reminding herself that Todd wasn't staying in Hickory Hollow.

Somehow she'd forgotten, between their conversation over coffee and working together to save Randy.

It had been a harsh reminder to hear him talking about the job waiting for him. He loved his work. And after seeing him with Randy, observing his quick thinking and efficient care that had meant the difference between life and death, she knew he must be good at his job.

Someone like Todd wouldn't be happy in a small town forever.

And he was an *Englisher*. She couldn't forget that.

Both things combined meant that, even if he

made her stomach flutter every time she got caught in the intensity of his gaze, even if she *liked* him, she had to guard her heart.

But he had offered to help her with the registration paperwork she still couldn't resolve, and she needed his help.

The clinic had back-to-back patients all morning and Todd was in his element.

There was a lull at lunchtime and they both finally looked up to catch their breaths.

Lena was finishing up wiping down one of the exam rooms when Todd appeared in the doorway.

He looked so handsome that for a moment her stomach twisted and she had to look down at her hands.

"Wouldn't you know, I forgot to bring my lunch again."

He sounded vaguely amused at himself.

"I know you've probably brought your own lunch, but would you mind terribly if I asked you to walk across to the restaurant and bring back something to eat? You should get something for yourself as well. I'm going to update a few patient charts that I didn't get to during the appointments."

He had a couple of bills in his hand where he leaned casually against the doorway.

"I don't mind." It would give her a moment to catch her breath out of his magnetizing presence.

"Any news on Mrs. Glick?" he asked when she moved through the doorway, brushing close to him.

She shook her head. "Not yet."

"If Hickory Hollow is anything like home, the baby will probably come in the middle of the night."

"You may be right." She'd woken in the night last night, sure she'd heard someone at the door. Everything had been quiet and still.

And it had taken her far too long to get back to sleep due to thoughts of Todd.

She slipped from the clinic out into the mid-morning air. Clouds scuttled across the sky and a breeze kissed her cheeks.

She crossed the street, mindful of the horse and buggy clopping down the street. That was Mr. Beiler and he waved to her in passing.

The doors of the library opened as her feet hit the sidewalk and Evan Miller exited the building with his teenage daughter.

"*Goot* morning," she said.

She meant to pass them by, but Evan stopped and she had no choice but to stop as well.

"How are you, Lena?"

"*Goot.* And you?"

Evan was a widower. His wife had died last year. He had five children, all daughters. Anna, the oldest, said a shy hello to Lena.

"Are you attending the singing next weekend?" Evan asked.

Lena blinked at him. "I'm not sure. Several babies are due to be born soon, and I have no way of knowing if one of the mothers will be at the center. Did you need a chaperone?"

Anna's eyes cut to her father, whose cheeks were tinged pink beneath his beard. How strange.

"Ah, no."

He didn't say anything else, and nerves shivered through Lena's belly. She glanced to the side and caught a glimpse of Todd, standing in the open doorway of the clinic, watching them. Had he forgotten to tell her something? Had she left the door open by accident?

"Were you heading to the library?" Evan asked, drawing her attention back to him.

"No." She smiled a bit, even though she felt unaccountably awkward. Probably because she sensed Todd still watching. "I'm helping at the clinic today, and the doctor asked me to grab a quick bite from the restaurant."

He seemed to deflate a bit at her answer.

"In fact, I'd better hurry in case the clinic gets busy again."

Evan and Anna said goodbye, and Lena made her way to the restaurant then back to the clinic.

The awkwardness of the encounter stuck with her. Was it because Todd had watched her the entire time?

Todd wasn't in the waiting area when she returned to the clinic. Lena heard movement from his office in the back and went into the kitchen to drop off Todd's food.

"I hope you bought something for yourself."

His voice from the doorway behind her startled her. She took a small Styrofoam container from the brown paper bag and moved so she was across the table from him when he entered the room.

"I treated myself to a piece of blueberry pie."

"Good."

He went to the sink to run a glass of water. "Did you run into a friend?"

He had seen her talking to Evan and Anna.

"That was Evan. He's a member of my church. A widower."

Why had she said that? Todd didn't need to know that information.

Todd turned from the sink, resting his hip casually against the counter. "What did he want?"

"He asked me whether I was going to next week's singing."

"What's a singing?"

She unpacked her lunch on the table, setting out the broccoli cheese soup in its container. She kept her eyes on what she was doing. "It's mostly for the single young people in our community. A chance to visit. Some will try to spend time with the—the person they are sweet on."

She glanced up in time to see a dark expression cross Todd's face, quickly gone. "Will you go?"

Her stomach dipped at his question. The same awkwardness she'd felt when Evan had asked her descended.

"Singings are for young people, not me."

"Why not you? You're single."

She stared at the table, not able to meet his eyes. "I'm well past the age when young men would be interested in courting me. I'll be a decade older than everyone at the singing. Or more."

He sputtered a little laugh and her eyes darted to him. He wore a smile but it didn't look particularly happy. He looked…frustrated somehow.

"You don't think your friend was asking about it because he wants to court you?"

She was certain the confusion and shock she felt must be showing on her face. "Evan? No."

"Then why did he ask?"

"I don't know! Probably because he wanted someone to keep an eye on his teenage daughter."

Todd shook his head. "I doubt it."

"You don't know him." *Or me.*

"So tell my why he wouldn't want to court you."

"Because I'm not marriage material," she blurted.

She hadn't meant to say that, and sudden tears pricked her eyes as the heat in her face grew to an inferno.

Todd looked shocked, his face pale and expression distressed. "Lena—"

But a voice from the waiting room called down the hall, interrupting whatever he would've said.

"I'll sign them in. You can grab a quick bite," she said. She rushed from the room, pressing cold hands to her hot cheeks.

Chapter Nine

Todd helped himself to a cup of coffee from the birthing center's kitchen.

Lena had been right when she'd told him that Jane Glick's baby would come today.

And he'd been right, too. This baby wanted to come in the middle of the night.

He'd been woken by a call to his cell phone. It'd been just after midnight and he'd been deeply asleep. He'd woken disoriented and half believing he was still dreaming, until Lena's voice through the line had anchored him.

"Jane is having her baby. Will you come?"

It had been a surreal experience, driving down the winding country roads so late at night. He'd been completely alone. No cars or buggies in sight.

When he'd arrived at Lena's center, it had

been lit up from within. Lamplight shone from every window.

Inside, the mother-to-be and her husband, Noah, were in one of the rooms. Jane's sister Sarai was also present, though she'd been busy in the next room, putting clean sheets on a crib with wheels, readying it for later.

Lena had met him in the hallway, her eyes alight, wearing a clean apron and carrying her chart of both Jane's vitals and the baby's heartbeat.

She was in her element.

And he wasn't at all sure he could do this.

He sipped his coffee, willing his hands to steady. He'd checked on Jane and said hello to her husband.

Both had been relaxed—as relaxed as a laboring mother could be—and the atmosphere inside the room was calm and clean.

But he was full of doubts. Todd excused himself and come in here to the kitchen.

Why had he thought he could do this? Every time he blinked, a memory of that terrible day in the ER burst forth.

The first patient he'd lost. Elise Tanner. She'd been a victim of a car accident and the trauma had caused her to go into early labor. There'd been so much blood…

And he hadn't been able to save her or her baby.

He'd been the one to notify her family, in the waiting room. The first person to see the devastation cross her husband's face. To see her mother burst into inconsolable sobs.

He'd had every tool and medicine available to him through the hospital, and it hadn't been enough.

Lena didn't even have a fetal monitor to strap across Jane's belly.

What if something went wrong?

"Everything all right?"

Lena's soft question from behind him startled him, and he set his mug on the counter with a loud *bang!*

He'd had his back to the door and turned to face her. "Fine." But he couldn't quite make himself smile.

Her gaze didn't quite meet his eyes.

"Jane was effaced at a nine. I'll check her again after I take her vitals."

She turned to go and he followed her out into the hallway.

He'd really put his foot in his mouth earlier today—or yesterday. It was already morning, though it was the dark of night.

I'm not marriage material. He hadn't meant to uncover an old wound. He'd been surprised by the awful, twisting feeling that had over-taken him when he'd watched her talking to Evan Miller on the sidewalk outside.

Jealousy.

He didn't consider himself to be a jealous person, but it had only gotten worse when she'd tried to explain what her supposed friend had wanted to talk about.

Miller had been interested in her. Todd was sure of that, even though she'd seemed oblivious.

When his conversation with Lena had been interrupted by a patient, and then another, she'd only murmured, *I don't want to talk about it* in passing.

He'd stewed on it all afternoon.

It wasn't his business and he *shouldn't* feel jealous.

But the logic he tried to apply didn't change how he felt.

She had a warm smile for Jane and Noah as she entered the room. He followed.

Sarai was nowhere to be seen, but he heard movement in the room next door. Still preparing.

"Still feeling all right?" Lena asked the mother-to-be.

Jane lay on her back in the bed, a sheet draped over her lower half.

"A little nauseous with the last two contractions," Noah said.

"There's nothing in my belly," Jane said. "I wasn't hungry for supper."

Lena patted her hand as she bent over the bed. "I've got some emesis bags right here, just in case. Mind if I take your blood pressure?"

At Jane's affirmative nod, Lena slipped the cuff over her arm. When a contraction came, Lena waited it out with the cuff loose and unfilled.

Sweat popped out on Jane's brow as she tried to breathe through the contraction.

Todd didn't watch. He went to the chart Lena had left on the counter and looked at the numbers. BP, temperature, heart rate, baby's heart rate. All were within a normal range.

It was too late for an ambulance to take Jane to the hospital for anything other than an extreme emergency. The stress of moving at this late stage would be worse for her.

Which meant Todd was going to deliver a baby.

He pushed away the terrible memories of his failure and prayed for peace. Felt the professional persona slip over him.

When he turned back around, Lena was listening to the baby's heartbeat with a fetoscope, a device similar to a stethoscope but with an end that curved so it could rest comfortable on a pregnant belly and pick up the baby's heartbeat better.

Lena said something quietly to Jane that Todd couldn't hear, then came to the counter to write on the chart.

He watched her scrawl the numbers on the page. The baby's heartbeat was slightly faster than the last reading. Still within an acceptable range. And Lena could've counted wrong. Human error was greater than that of a machine.

"It won't be long now," Lena said softly to him. "I'm going to ask Sarai to wash up."

It was a gentle reminder that he should do the same. There was a sink built into the counter farther down from where they stood.

He crossed behind her as she flipped a page and made notes on the paper beneath.

He turned on the water, thankful that it would drown out the sound of his voice, at least a little. He didn't want Jane or Noah to hear.

"We never got to finish our conversation earlier," he murmured. And she seemed determined to avoid being alone with him. She'd scurried out of the kitchen only moments ago. He couldn't keep this inside any longer.

She sent him a scathing sideways glance. "Now isn't the time."

"Why not? What I have to say won't take long." He pumped soap from the dispenser next to the sink and began to scrub his hands and wrists. "Whoever told you that you weren't marriage material was wrong."

She had her head down, though her pencil had stopped its movement across the page. She was listening.

"You're intelligent and capable and kind and compassionate." *And beautiful.*

Something inside him sensed that it would be too much to say the last.

"Whoever he was, he was a fool."

Lena should never have allowed Todd to distract her.

You're intelligent and capable and kind and compassionate.

His words of praise had lit her up inside, soothed old hurts that she'd thought long ago scarred over.

He hadn't called her beautiful. And maybe it meant she could believe his compliments. She knew she was plain. She'd always known she couldn't compare to her sisters.

She'd busied her hands with small, last-minute tasks.

She'd come in to take Jane's vitals for what

she thought would be the last time. When she listened to the baby's heartbeat through the fetoscope, it was flying far too fast.

Todd. She didn't know for sure whether she'd said his name or just thought it, but he looked up from where he was speaking to Sarai near the door.

"The baby's heartbeat is too fast."

It could mean a complication.

Todd moved to the end of the bed. "Should we call for an ambulance?"

"I want to try something," she said. Then, to Jane, "I know it hurts, but I need you to shift to your left side. Noah, can you help her?"

Lena moved out of the way, as Jane groaned and worked to roll onto her side. Lena took an extra pillow from the bed and put it between Jane's knees.

Another contraction came and Jane cried out.

A glance at Todd showed his lips were pinched, the skin around his eyes tight.

Noah moved to Jane's head and Lena slipped back in beside her, using the fetoscope again.

Swish swish, swish swish.

She listened carefully, the moment prolonged as the baby's heartbeat returned to a normal rate.

"He or she is all right. The heartbeat is settling back to normal." The change in position must have helped renew the blood flow to the unborn baby.

Todd met her gaze, something shifting behind his eyes.

He came to stand beside her, and when she would've moved, he placed his fingers over hers where she held the fetoscope. His other hand extended, a silent request.

She disengaged the earpieces and passed him the fetoscope—but he didn't let her go.

He was so close that their shoulders bumped. She could feel the coiled tension inside him.

He cared.

About Jane and the baby.

He must've heard the same steady heartbeat that she had, because some of the tension left him.

She hadn't realized she was holding her breath until he let go of her and she exhaled shakily. They both straightened and she moved away quickly, before anyone else registered the tension between them.

"I—" Jane huffed, another contraction straining her muscles. "Need to. Push."

Lena let her eyes scan the room once more. Noah knelt on the floor just in front of Jane, holding her hands. Sarai had been a patient at the center before and had helped Lena a few times. She was ready with some toweling in her hands.

Lena had set out a tray with the implements they might need. Forceps—rarely used—umbilical scissors to cut the cord, needle and thread for after.

They were ready.

It didn't take long. Only minutes for a new life to be born. Todd caught the baby, carefully handing off the boy to Lena. The baby cried as she wiped his face clean, then quickly handed him to his mama, who was openly weeping. Noah had tears in his eyes.

Lena loved watching parents in those first moments, welcoming their new little one into the world. She found herself a little misty.

Soon enough, she helped Jane deliver the placenta then assisted Sarai as she bathed the baby. Todd, meanwhile, examined Jane and put in a few stitches.

And then there was only the cleanup left, and that was accomplished quickly enough thanks to years of practice.

She loaded up the two washing machines in the mudroom off the back of the center. There was a deep sink there, with a little window above it, and Lena stopped for a moment to strip off her apron and wash up.

From here, she could see only the outline of trees across her yard and a slice of the night sky. Everything was quiet and dark. The stars sparkled on their velvet tapestry.

Lena was tired in the best way possible. She always felt this sense of accomplishment, of peace, after helping a new mother through a birth.

But tonight, there was something different. Todd.

He had addled her from the beginning. She was attracted to him.

But this was more.

She'd thought she was happy with her quiet life running the birthing center. Until he'd arrived and threw everything out of whack.

He was an *Englisher*. An intelligent man who questioned everything. And his questions had made her wonder about her own long-held beliefs.

She dried her hands on a towel, still watching the quiet night outside.

Mamm was the one who'd first said Lena wasn't marriage material. But would Lena really be happy without a family of her own?

Todd's words had shaken free what she'd believed for so long. She didn't know whether he was right, that Evan Miller had been interested in her. That she could one day have a family of her own, with Evan or someone else. John's rejection from so long ago remained an echo in her heart.

What did she truly want?

Todd.

The answer came quickly, and she dismissed it just the same way.

She crossed the room to the linen cabinet and pulled out a clean apron. She slipped it over her head, the weight of it on her neck as she tied it behind her a reminder of their differences.

Todd didn't belong in Hickory Hollow. Lena would grow old here. It was her home.

They didn't have a future.

Maybe she couldn't help her mind jumping to him when she thought of a future with a husband and children, but she could control the thoughts that came after.

Todd wasn't for her.

Even if he'd opened up something inside her.

Made her hope again.

Hope.

That's what it was, this terrifying, exhilarating bubble inside her.

She'd given up her hopes for a family of her own. Now they were reignited.

She could be thankful of that, even if Todd would never be a part of that future.

She had been wary of letting their friendship grow, but Todd had surprised her with his kindness and willingness to learn. She would let their friendship grow and flourish.

As long as she didn't fall in love with him.

Chapter Ten

Lena was scrambling some eggs at the stove in the center's kitchen when Todd appeared in the kitchen doorway and leaned his shoulder into the jamb.

"Hungry?" he asked with a bemused smile on his lips.

"No, but Jane is." It was only ninety minutes after the birth. The new mother had already been up and out of bed to use the restroom. Noah had stayed in the room to watch over the babe they'd named Levi, while Lena had helped Jane shuffle slowly into the restroom and back into bed.

"Do you often cook in the middle of the night for your patients?" Todd sounded curious, and a glance at him showed his intense gaze resting on her.

"When it's needed."

She always did what was needed. Whether that was fetching extra blankets, helping a brand-new mother feed her baby for the first time, or cooking something.

"How did you know?" he asked quietly after a glance over his shoulder. Sarai had gone home, so perhaps he was making sure neither Jane nor Noah had come out into the hall to hear him.

"Know what?"

"That the baby's heartbeat would stabilize once Jane turned over."

She considered the question as she added steaming eggs to the plate she'd already prepared on a wooden tray, out on the counter. Two pieces of toast waited. She had small dishes of butter and jam, along with tiny salt and pepper shakers and a napkin and silverware arranged artfully on the tray as well.

"A…feeling, I suppose. I've done the same before. There've been a few rare times when the baby was in distress and I had to call for an ambulance to take mother and baby to the hospital. Doc Bradshaw and I always try—tried," she corrected herself, "not to let it get to that point. We send patients to the hospital as early as we can, if there are signs that a home birth isn't ideal."

His expression was considering as she picked up the tray and moved toward him. He stepped into the room to let her pass into the hallway.

After she delivered the abbreviated meal, she took vitals for mother and baby and charted them.

She suspected that after Jane got some food in her belly, she would want to sleep. She certainly deserved it.

Lena was a light sleeper and, like her *aendi* before her, she'd learned to wake up when the baby cried. *Aendi* Carol had taught her it was better to check on the new mothers and babies when they were awake, rather than waking them up to take their temperature and use the blood pressure cuff.

Whenever there was a new baby, Lena always experienced a few sleepless nights.

And she loved every minute of it.

She returned to the kitchen to clean up, only to find Todd had gathered her pan and spatula by the sink.

"You don't have to clean up," she said. "I'll wash the dishes after Jane is finished."

"All right." He ran one hand through his hair,

and she couldn't help noticing the breadth of his shoulders.

She cut her eyes away. Her gaze landed on the darkened window.

"You don't have to stay," she said. "Doc Bradshaw usually didn't." The clinic would be open tomorrow, and Todd should catch a few hours of sleep before he was expected to doctor anyone.

He started to say something, then changed his mind. He half turned and tipped his head to indicate the papers spread across the small table in the nook at the back of the room.

"Is this the paperwork you've been working on?"

She still had a slight buzz of adrenaline from delivering Jane's baby, but she sighed at his question. "Yes. I'm muddling through."

He walked over to the table and glanced down at the top paper, which was mostly information about the center. "I made a few calls this afternoon, after you'd left the clinic."

He had? She hadn't forgotten his agreement to help her, but she'd been unsettled by what had passed between them at lunchtime and had rushed out of the clinic so she wouldn't be alone with Todd.

She'd acted like a foolish schoolgirl.

She was a little embarrassed about it, even now. She busied her hands, wetting a cloth at the sink and wiping down the countertops.

"Alexander Huffman is the director who signs off on all the hospital registrations," she told him. "Do you know him?"

"I had never spoken with him before today."

Todd had been able to track down Mr. Huffman?

"What about your aunt? Was she ever in contact with him?"

"I can't recall *Aendi* Carol ever mentioning someone by that name."

His long fingers trailed over the top of her papers. His focus remained on the table. Was he reading her application?

"I think he knew you. Or at least, he knew *of* you. When I said I was calling about the Amish birthing center, he didn't give me any answers and seemed in a hurry to end the call. At least that was my impression."

She rinsed out her washcloth, wrung it out and put it away. "I'm certain I've never met the man. I can ask around. Maybe my *mamm* or another relative might know whether *Aendi* Carol had a connection to him."

She turned around to find him staring at her. One hand was in his pocket, the fingertips of the other still resting on the table. His eyes were warm and a little sleepy.

And her stomach dipped precipitously.

"And those—" she pointed to the papers on the table "—are a worry for another day. You should go home and sleep."

He shook his head, but his feet carried him closer, until he was even with her.

"I'm not sure I can sleep," he admitted.

He was taller than her and she had to tip her head back a bit to see his face. "What do you do in your emergency room if you work an overnight shift?"

His eyes smiled at her before his lips did. "There is a room with several cots. If I get the chance, I usually lie there and stare at the ceiling."

She shook her head a little but couldn't keep the responding smile from her lips.

"I like it when you smile at me."

His husky words, spoken in a near whisper, released a horde of butterflies inside her.

She hadn't realized she was leaning toward him until his hand came to her waist to steady her.

Had they already been standing this close?

His smile was nowhere to be seen now. She was the recipient of his full focus, and it made her light-headed to be regarded with that intent stare.

Was he—

His gaze lowered to her lips, then flicked back to her eyes.

She couldn't help but echo the movement. What would it be like, to have Todd kiss her just once?

The thought shocked her out of the moment. What was she doing?

She turned away, turning so that his hand fell away from her side. She brushed one hand across her blazing cheek.

"I think you should go." She couldn't look at him.

Had he seen her foolish thoughts reflected in her expression? She couldn't bear it if he laughed at her.

Although…he'd seemed to be caught up in the moment with her.

Her whirling thoughts wouldn't settle, and she grabbed the counter to steady herself.

"I'm sorry," came his voice from behind her.

"There's nothing—nothing to be sorry for." Her hand fluttered at her side without her conscious thought. "It's late and we were both caught up in the moment. It's been an exciting night."

She'd had other exciting nights working alongside Doc Bradshaw. Once, there'd been three babies born here within a few hours of each other.

And she'd never wanted to kiss Doc Bradshaw.

Nothing had happened.

She repeated it to herself as she heard his footsteps retreat toward the door.

Where they stopped.

He spoke, his voice a little hesitant. "Is it… all right if I come and check on Jane and the baby in the morning?"

"Of course!" She made her voice bright.

But she still couldn't turn and look at him, not when her cheeks were burning with the hottest blush she'd ever felt.

And not when she still wanted his kiss so badly.

We were both caught up in the moment.

Lena's words rolled around in Todd's head.

He sat in his car, in the dark, in the dead of night, staring at Lena's birthing center.

He'd almost kissed her.

The way she'd looked at him…he'd been sure they were on the same page.

And then she'd backed away.

He didn't know whether it was against some

Amish rule for her to kiss him. And there was no way he was bringing this up with David.

Caught up in the moment.

Had he been?

He'd known exhilaration. There'd been patients that he'd brought back from the brink of death.

This wasn't the same. But she'd given him an out, an excuse for what had almost happened.

He liked her. He liked her a lot.

Tonight had shown him what it would be like for the doctor who came to operate the clinic on a permanent basis.

He and Lena had been perfectly in sync. When he'd wanted a clean towel, she'd handed him one before he'd opened his mouth to ask.

She was efficient in taking vitals and she'd kept him apprised at all times.

She'd been at his shoulder as he'd caught Levi Glick in his hands. He didn't think she'd seen the tears he'd quickly blinked away.

He'd witnessed a baby's birth tonight and it had been miraculous. Nothing like his experiences in the ER.

There'd been a sense of peace and calmness with Lena there in the room. It wasn't only the atmosphere of the center, the warm, welcoming feel of it compared to a hospital's clinical state. It was Lena's capable presence extending beyond herself and touching him and Jane and everyone else in the room.

He'd never felt anything like it before.

That's what he'd been caught up in.

It was Lena.

And he wanted nothing more than to get out of his car and storm back inside, take her in his arms and kiss her.

His hands flexed on the steering wheel.

He would love to work with her in an ongoing capacity. After tonight, how could he go back to working with a random rotation of nurses? Sure, whoever they were, they'd be professional and compassionate.

But they wouldn't be Lena.

There was a part of him that could see a future working alongside Lena. Letting their friendship blossom into something more. Delivering babies and helping the people in this county.

From the console, his phone buzzed with a notification. New email.

The sound was a wake-up call. What was he doing? One great night delivering a baby and he was dreaming about staying in little Hickory Hollow?

His mouth twisted in a wry smirk. He picked up his phone and tapped to see the email.

It was from his boss, informing him of a meet and greet scheduled for his first day, a chance to get to know the doctors, nurses and staff he'd be working with at Lakeview Barrett.

Todd put the phone down, blinking away the haze left from looking at the screen in the dark.

He had a path. One that Grandfather had crafted for him and one that Todd had agreed to before he'd even graduated high school.

We've had a doctor in every generation. Grandfather had uttered those words to Todd on the eve of his fifteenth birthday. *I think it should be you.*

He'd been proud to be the recipient of Grandfather's praise. The man never said or did anything without a purpose.

And he'd also heard an echo of Grandfather's snarl when he'd disowned cousin Tyler.

Grandfather had believed in Todd. Pushed him, on the rare occasion during med school when Todd had thought about giving up.

Grandfather had expectations. So did Todd's new boss and the hospital board.

So did Todd. He liked the life he had in Columbus. Lena had shown him that maybe he hadn't taken enough time for his family, but he could rectify that. At least, to a degree.

He wouldn't be happy here in the long term, would he? It was so slow in this tiny town. It was almost as if he'd stepped back in time.

Maybe he was infatuated with Lena right now, but could that last? They were so different.

She challenged him in ways no one else did. That was part of it.

But it would never work. Not when he had a future in Columbus, and hers was here.

He wanted her friendship. What had happened between them tonight couldn't happen again. He couldn't risk losing her friendship and she'd gone all shy about what had happened.

He'd be careful when they were together. But there was no way he could stay away from her, not when she brought so much light to his time here.

Chapter Eleven

"You really do all this every time you go somewhere?" Todd asked.

Lena looked up from where she was buckling one side of the horse's harness. They were behind the small barn on her property, set away from the center itself.

She and Todd were buckling her horse into the harness to go for a ride in the buggy. A week had passed since they'd delivered Jane's baby. Two days after Jane had given birth, Emma Rober had delivered her baby during the early afternoon. There'd been no complications, and Lena had witnessed Todd experiencing the miracle of birth all over again.

He hadn't tried to kiss her this time. There'd been a quick, joyful hug as he'd rushed out of the center—he'd left a waiting room full of patients behind.

When he'd come to check on Mama and Baby later in the evening, after he'd seen the remainder of his patients, he'd brought food from the Amish restaurant. Lasagna, her favorite. And he'd brought enough for Emma and her husband, too. It had been thoughtful, and Lena had been touched. Todd had stayed to eat with her in the tiny kitchen nook, telling her about the patients he'd seen that day.

He'd come back again the next day for a final check of the new mother and her daughter. He'd stayed for an extra half hour and helped Lena hang washed sheets and blankets on the clothesline outside.

She'd seen him again at house church two days later. He'd made sure to come to her for a catch-up, though he and his family had eaten separately. He'd mentioned that his brother David was teasing him about not being able to drive a buggy.

When she'd suggested that *she* could teach him, he'd lit up.

And so here they were.

Where the idea had come from, she didn't know. The words had popped out of her mouth before she'd thought them through.

This friendship between her and Todd was growing. That's all it was.

But friendship didn't explain the way her heart had leaped when she'd heard his car pull up outside a bit ago.

It also didn't explain why she'd chosen to wear her best dress, the one she usually reserved for Sunday worship. The dark rose color was her favorite.

"I didn't realize I was going to get the full experience today," he said. His eyes were sparkling at her over the horse's back. He wore a casual outfit of jeans and a finely woven shirt that hugged his shoulders. It happened to be a dark blue that complemented the sky blue of his eyes.

"It's all part of the deal." She patted the horse's neck and moved around to Todd's side to check that the buckles were secure.

And Todd lifted one speaking eyebrow. "Checking my work?"

"I have no desire for the horse to be injured. Or us. I don't want to be hurt."

He'd gone serious. "I don't want that, either."

She found herself caught in his stare and blinked to break the connection. She must be careful. Todd was a friend. He could only ever be a friend. She mustn't assign meaning to his words that weren't there. They were talking about the buggy ride and that was all.

Feeling a bit steadier, she gestured to the buggy. "Let's climb in."

His hand was warm as he handed her into the buggy first. Her stomach flipped at the touch, a simple friendly gesture.

She forced a calming breath in through her nose and out through her mouth and prayed that he hadn't noticed her reaction.

She showed him the brake pedal and explained how to use it. He released his foot and the buggy became loose. Ready to move.

"The horse has been pulling a buggy for almost as long as you've been practicing medicine," she said. "He knows what to do."

"Really? He's that old?" Todd sent her a sideways look. "Somehow that doesn't make me feel better."

"You drive a car that goes much faster than Old John, here, but you're frightened?"

His hands clasped the reins in his lap tightly, then relaxed. "My car is reinforced steel and protective glass." He gave an exaggerated glance around the open buggy. "There's nothing protecting us if we get in an accident."

Her lips twitched with amusement she tried to hide. "So don't get in an accident."

He shot her a look. "Thank you for your advice," he said dryly.

Now she did let a smile break free. "I won't let you get hurt."

When he still didn't relax, she said, "We'll stick to the quiet back roads. No highways today."

He snorted. "There isn't a single highway in this county."

She clucked at the horse and gave the command, "Let's go," and the buggy lurched beneath them as the horse began to walk.

Old John was well trained and knew how to cross her yard and join the road. Todd didn't even have to do anything with the reins.

Which was a good thing. His shoulders were strung with tension, and he was holding the reins so tightly his knuckles stood out white against his skin. Thank goodness there was enough slack that the horse wasn't bothered.

"You have to relax," she said over the buggy's creaking and the rattle of its wheels.

Todd shook his head tightly. "I'm not sure I can."

The horse began to trot, because she always trotted him on this straight, open stretch of road.

Todd jumped. "You'd better distract me."

She laughed a little. "How?"

"Has Evan Miller come calling?"

"No." The wind blew fine strands of her hair against her cheek and she brushed them back.

"Would you go for a buggy ride with him if he did?"

"I don't know," she answered honestly.

Did Todd know that buggy rides were one way Amish couples courted? A long drive together was a time to talk, get to know each other, maybe even hold hands.

She kept her hands hidden in the folds of her apron.

Even if Todd knew about this particular Amish custom, that wasn't why they were here today. They were friends. She was teaching him to drive a buggy. That was all.

She hadn't given Evan Miller another thought since that day outside the clinic. Evan didn't make her insides quake and her pulse flutter like being near Todd did.

"If you ever get married, will you still be able to run the center?"

"I have no plans to get married," she said stiffly.

"I'm not trying to hurt your feelings." He glanced at her, and she thought maybe he was trying to gauge if he had. He didn't focus on her for long, quickly returning his eyes to the road. "It was more of a rhetorical question. When

I was a kid, I remember this one book that was assigned to us in school. It had a female schoolteacher in it, and when she got married, she wasn't allowed to teach anymore. I'm still learning about your ways. I guess I was wondering if that happened in your community."

So he wasn't asking about her specifically. She thought for a moment. "I suppose it would depend on my—hypothetical—husband. Many married Amish women work from their homes. Like this."

She gestured to the upcoming farm. A fence ran alongside the road and up ahead was a large slab of wood made into a crude hand-painted sign that read "Quilts."

"Your work is a lot more involved than piecing together quilts," he said quietly.

It wasn't a compliment, not really, but it warmed her anyway.

"You've obviously never tried to make a quilt," she teased lightly. "They can be complicated. And Jenny is talented."

"Should we stop?"

He sounded tense just making the suggestion. Which probably meant he was nervous.

And it would be good practice for him to learn stopping and starting the buggy.

"Yes. Let's stop for a visit."

* * *

Todd's gut was tight as Lena instructed him how to slow down and turn the horse into the gravel driveway.

He didn't quail at driving his own car at high speeds on the interstate, but right now he felt like he was sixteen again, behind the wheel of his father's sedan. Sweaty palms, queasy feeling in his stomach, pounding pulse and everything.

Or maybe part of it was sitting next to Lena. Especially when he'd asked her about Miller.

He must have used the reins incorrectly, because Lena reached over. Her slender fingers clasped his wrist and guided it more to the left.

Her touch sent prickles of awareness zinging up and down his spine. Ones that he did his best to ignore.

He breathed a sigh of relief when the horse slowed and stopped in the wide dirt-packed space between a one-story house and barn. The house had a quaint porch along one side, but after he'd set the brake and they'd climbed down, Lena led him around the side of the house, not to the porch. There was a large room that must've been added on to the house at some point. A handmade sign in a small window proclaimed the shop was open.

Lena opened the door and he followed her inside.

"Jenny?" Lena called out.

Stepping inside was like stepping into a different world. Quilts hung from display racks on the walls. Some huge, large enough to fit a king-size bed. Some smaller, made for twins or full beds. And some that might be made for a baby bed or to cover a lap.

There were simple designs and intricate, spectacular ones. Soft colors and bright colors. This wasn't only quilting. This was artwork. And lots of it. Standing racks took up space in the center of the room, making rows of quilts upon quilts.

A woman who might've been his mother's age emerged from inside the house through a door. Beyond her, he could see a homey kitchen, similar in feel to the one at David and Ruby's home.

Lena made introductions all around.

"Are you looking for something in particular?" Jenny asked.

He didn't miss her curious, sharp gaze. No doubt she was wondering what he was doing here with Lena.

"We're just browsing for a bit," Lena said.

"Actually, my mother's birthday is coming

up," he said. "She'd love a beautiful quilt like this."

Jenny smiled and left them to browse, making sure he knew she was nearby if he needed help choosing.

He'd settled on a geometric flower-style design that he didn't know the name of and within a few minutes, they were in the buggy again.

He tried releasing some of his pent-up tension with a big breath. It didn't quite work.

Lena helped get them back on the road. She glanced his way, then bent to pull something from the storage space beneath their feet. A small picnic basket.

"Here."

She offered him a sugar cookie.

But he had the reins in his hands.

She seemed to sense his dilemma and gathered the reins into one of his hands. "We're on a straight stretch here," she explained.

The cookie melted on his tongue. "How'd you know I would be hungry?"

"You're always hungry. I've got apple slices and some cheese from a local farm."

Had she been thinking about him? She must've, to pack away a snack. He liked it.

He finished the cookie and reached for his

phone in his pocket. But when he patted his pocket, it was empty.

"I left my phone in the car," he realized. He remembered glancing at his emails before he'd driven to Lena's place and tossing the phone into the passenger seat. He'd been in such a rush to see her, he hadn't remembered to grab it.

"How will you ever survive?" she teased in a droll voice.

"Hey." He softened the protest with a smile. "I was going to read you an email I got. I can't believe I forgot about it until now. I finally heard from Alexander Huffman."

She brightened and he wished he would've cautioned her before he'd started.

"He knew about the center. He wrote back that his daughter had quote *turned Amish* and wanted to have her baby there. She died two years ago."

Lena looked at him with wide, sad eyes. She turned her face to stare at the fields they were passing. "Dorothy," she murmured.

"You knew her?"

"Yes. Her husband, Isaiah, was friends with my younger sister."

The sadness in her voice unmanned him.

He tried to copy what she'd shown him before and reined in the horse so they were standing on the empty stretch of road. He didn't like sitting out here in the open, but there were fields on both sides. Surely anybody driving down this road would see the large black buggy and horse on the road.

He turned to her. "I'm sorry, Lena."

When she turned her face to him, he saw her eyes were red, though she wasn't crying. "Dorothy was one of my patients." She took a shuddering breath. "She was several years younger than me. I knew she had *Englisher* parents. She met her husband, Isaiah, during his *rumpshpringa* when he was sixteen. He'd moved to the city for a few months and that's how they met. When he decided to return home, she came with him. They were both young, and they were happy together..."

She dipped her head and plucked at her apron. "She had symptoms of preeclampsia. Doc Bradshaw and I advised her that she should have her baby at the hospital."

His surprise must've shown on his face. She glanced at him then back down. "I care about my patients," she said, her voice husky with unshed tears.

"Dorothy was set against a hospital birth. She seemed almost frightened of it. I wonder..." She shook her head, her voice trailing off.

"What?" He didn't mean to, but his hand closed over hers on her lap.

She stilled for a moment, and then her hand curled into his so she was holding on to him, too.

"I knew she was estranged from her parents. I wonder if that's why she was so against an *Englisher* hospital. Doc and I called an ambulance, but it was too late…" She sniffed and wiped her face with her other hand. "We lost the baby, too."

And Lena was still mourning it.

He squeezed her hand gently. "Sometimes patients go against doctor's orders." He'd seen it, enough times to know that one couldn't force their patient to choose what was best for their own health. But Lena had been affected by it. Was still affected by it, thanks to Dorothy's father.

"I will write to him," she said. "Do you think that would help? I could list the patients who've had healthy babies. Explain about our procedures. Would you sign it, if I wrote a letter like that?"

He hesitated and she drew her hand away. He felt like he'd lost something.

"I don't know how much it will help," he said. "I won't be here for much longer. It might be better to have your letter cosigned by the doctor who gets hired for the clinic long term."

She smiled stiffly. "Of course." She glanced away.

"Lena—" How did he even explain this?

"We should get going," she said with a false brightness. "If we turn right at the next corner, it's another mile to circle back home."

"Lena." He didn't reach for her again, but waited until she gave him her eyes. "I have family expectations. My grandfather started the emergency program at the Lakeview Barrett hospital. He paved the way for me to work there. It's a huge honor and I—" He'd wanted this new job, planned for it.

But he hated the way shadows chased behind her eyes. "Of course I understand. I feel the same way about the center. My *aendi* left a legacy and I can't give it up." Her smile trembled. "I'll find a way to fight for the center."

Chapter Twelve

Friday afternoon, a handful of days later, Lena was helping out at the clinic again. Mrs. Smith had needed to visit a family friend for the day.

There were a few patients left, including her own *aendi* Kate, whom Lena had encouraged to see the new doctor. Lena was worried her *aendi* might need surgery on the opposite foot.

She could hear Todd's voice in the second exam room, a low, familiar rumble that never failed to make her heart beat just slightly faster.

He was finishing up with a mother and daughter, while she cleaned and sanitized this exam room and brought back the next patient.

She couldn't help a glance down the hall, toward the tiny kitchenette, when she left the exam room. Today, she'd come prepared with extra portions of her leftover roast and potatoes and veggies, only to find that Todd had asked Mrs. Schrock to prepare a meal for them both. They'd been too busy today to sit down together, but they'd passed by each other and shared smiles while grabbing a bite when they could.

And Todd had murmured, "Maybe when we're done for the day, we can heat up your roast and catch up."

She wanted that. Wanted to sit across from him at the little table and share about her week, her upcoming patients, find out whether he'd had time to visit David and Ruby and his nieces.

She hadn't decided whether she was going to tell him about visiting Isaiah Speicher. Yesterday, she'd gone to ask for the young man's help. To find out whether he might reach out to Huffman on her behalf.

Isaiah had been sorry to hear about the troubles she was having, but had refused to speak to Huffman. He had been kind in his refusal.

And she couldn't blame him. He was still grieving, two years after Dorothy had died.

She wasn't sure what to do now.

And this moment wasn't the time to think about it.

When she returned to the waiting area to bring back the next patient, an older couple who hadn't been there the last time she'd brought back a patient, was standing on one side of the room. An *Englisher* couple. How interesting. Lena's community was mostly Amish, but Todd did see the occasional *Englisher* in his practice.

She sighed. One more patient meant at least fifteen more minutes added on to the length of time they'd be here tonight—Todd wouldn't turn anyone away.

But she put on a pleasant smile and motioned them to meet her at the check-in desk.

The older woman, who appeared to be about the same age as Lena's mother and was dressed up in slacks and a silk blouse, wasn't paying attention. Her eyes darted around the room as she took in the patients and the room itself.

The man with her—her husband?—had salt-and-pepper hair and was dressed just as nicely. As if they'd come from an *Englisher* Sunday worship service. He had been watching Lena since she entered the room and nudged his wife in the direction of the check-in desk.

"How can I help you today?" Lena asked with a smile. "Do you need to see the doctor?"

"Why, yes." The woman shared a secret smile with her husband.

Lena reached for one of the clipboards kept on the side of the desk, ready with blank New

Patient paperwork. "We have a few patients before Doctor Todd will be able to see you—"

"Mom? Dad?"

She hadn't heard Todd coming down the hall behind her, so his words surprised her. He said goodbye to Esther Raber and her daughter Faith, then approached the couple standing at the desk.

He smiled broadly. "What are you doing here? I thought you were coming down tomorrow for the farmers' market."

Todd's mother embraced him first. "We decided to come down a half day early."

"Your mother booked that little B and B she's been itching to try." His father moved in as his wife stepped back. Neither man seemed ashamed of the emotion on the older man's face as he patted Todd's shoulder and then stepped back.

"We wanted to surprise you," Todd's mother said.

"I'm surprised!"

Lena realized she was intruding on their private moment, staring as she was.

She dipped her head and let her eyes scan the top of the desk. On the left side, opposite the New Patient paperwork, were the clipboards with documents that had already been filled out. She'd take the next patient back and take vitals while Todd had a moment with his parents.

But he stopped her with a hand on her arm as she was picking up the clipboard. "Mom, Dad, I want you to meet Lena Hochstetler. She's become something of my right-hand gal. At least, when we get to work together."

Lena flushed at his unexpected compliment.

"Lena, this is my mom and dad, Kimberly and Michael."

"It's lovely to meet you." She extended her hand, which both Barretts eagerly shook. She didn't miss the way Kimberly's curious gaze skipped from her to Todd and back again.

"Lena runs the birthing center I was telling you about. She's filling in today in Mrs. Smith's absence."

"She certainly has a welcoming presence," Michael said to Todd.

Lena's blush burned hotter.

Kimberly patted Todd's arm. "We won't keep you, dear. I know you have more patients to see."

That was Lena's cue to take her leave. She grabbed the top clipboard and clutched it to her stomach, ready to slip past Todd where he stood beside the desk, but again he halted her with a hand to her wrist.

"Can you join us for dinner tonight?" Michael asked Todd. "The restaurant across the street looks good."

"It is good," Todd said easily. His gaze shifted to Lena and seemed laced with apology. "Maybe we can share that pot roast another time?"

"You should join us," Kimberly blurted. Her eyes went wide as if she was surprised at herself. Her husband seemed a tiny bit confused, and Todd was watching her with narrowed eyes. "We'd love to get to know you. I know Todd has benefited from your friendship."

"I—" She didn't know what to say and sent a beseeching gaze to Todd. She didn't want to interrupt his time with his parents. She knew he hadn't seen them often these past weeks, and he'd probably see them even less once he started his new position.

She should say no. Right?

But his eyes were warm and crinkled a little at the corners like they did at the beginning of one of his smiles.

"You should come. You deserve a nice supper after I've run you ragged all day."

She didn't feel like that at all. The clinic had a different pace than the center, but she didn't mind being busy. She and Todd were helping people.

"I can stay."

"It's settled then," Kimberly said warmly. "We'll see you both after you wrap up for the day." She and Michael breezed out of the clinic, which was when Lena registered the curious eyes on her from *Aendi* Kate and her sister Julie, who'd brought her in.

She'd mentioned the temporary doctor to her family, of course. But this...having *Aendi* Kate and Julie witness the warm interaction with Todd's parents meant that she was going to have some explaining to do the next time she went home to share a meal.

If only she knew how to explain things to herself.

The Amish restaurant was busier than usual when Todd and Lena arrived after closing up the clinic.

Todd ushered Lena inside with a hand at the middle of her back. Partly to keep her from turning away to leave.

She'd tried to get out of the dinner briefly as they'd cleaned the exam room together after the last patient had left. She'd made an excuse that he should spend the time with his parents alone. He'd reminded her that she'd been invited and that she'd accepted.

A part of him wondered whether she had felt pressured to accept, with his parents there watching and a waiting room full of curious people behind them.

Didn't she want to spend the time with him?

Because lately he'd found himself counting down the hours until he could see her again. She'd given him a list of three women who could go into labor at any time and the only thing he could think was, *Good.* Then he'd be able to spend time with her. Even working by her side was enough to light up his entire day.

"There they are." He nodded his head toward the booth against the restaurant's back wall. Mom must've been watching, because she waved at them, her expression bright and excited.

He and Lena began threading their way through the other tables toward Mom and Dad.

A booth was intimate. It meant sitting closer than they would've at a table, thanks to Mom and Dad already sitting on one side.

He squelched the sneaky joy that rose inside him at that thought.

When Lena had scooted in to the booth and Todd had sat down beside her, Mom reached across the table to squeeze his hand.

"I'm glad you could make time for us," Mom

said. "We didn't meant to interrupt your date night."

"Oh, we're not dating," Lena rushed to say.

He'd recognized Mom's way of fishing for information, but Lena's quick refusal still pinched.

He affected a casual smile. "We're—"

"We're coworkers," Lena said at the same time.

"—friends," he finished a beat after her. The word seemed to echo in the sudden silence over the table.

Lena caught his questioning glance even as her fingers played with the edge of the silverware lying on the table.

He didn't want her to be nervous. So he nudged her foot with his beneath the table, where no one else could see.

He winked at her.

"Lena took pity on me when I first arrived," he said to his parents.

"I didn't take pity on you." Her words were shy and her eyes downcast, but he sensed her relaxing the slightest bit.

"No, I guess not." He tipped his head toward his dad. "She called me out on my bedside manner."

Dad chuckled. "Gotta like a gal who gives it

to you straight." Dad tapped the menu on the table in front of him. "Do you need a minute to look over this?"

"No, I like the potpie."

"The potpie is his favorite." Lena's words overlapped his.

If they had been trying to convince his parents there was nothing between them, they'd failed. And quickly, too.

Mom's eyes danced, and he knew there was no way she'd missed the interplay between them. Oh well. He wasn't ashamed of his deepening friendship with Lena.

He was starting to wish that they could be something more.

Their waitress, Lovina, a woman Todd recognized, took orders, then returned to the kitchen.

"I tried calling you on our drive down," Dad said. "To let you know our change of plans. You didn't answer."

"I left my phone in my office today. It was on silent. I didn't hear it." Todd had seen the notification for his dad's missed call, and one from his grandfather, when he'd collected his phone just before he and Lena had left the clinic.

Dad's brows crunched together. "That's not like you."

Todd shrugged. "It was a busy day. Not a lot of time for checking emails." He couldn't say whether his subconscious had made him forget his phone on the desk or whether it had been an oversight.

Dad let it go with only a raised eyebrow. Todd figured he might hear about it again later tonight, after Lena had left. Todd always had his phone at hand.

Maybe Lena had been right back at the beginning, when they'd had that first coffee together.

He'd been too self-absorbed. Or at least absorbed in the virtual life his phone provided.

He hadn't realized until he'd picked it up again how much of a relief it had been not to be tied to the device all day. He hadn't felt the urge to check messages. He'd been focused solely on the people in front of him, on their needs. There'd been several patients, like Asher Stoltzfus, whom he'd seen several times in the past weeks. He'd been able to chat with the man about his crop and his children.

His dependency on—or independence from—his phone would change when he moved back to the city. His colleagues would expect him to be available by text or call at all times. The nurses, too.

And things with his patients would differ as well. He didn't see many recurring patients in the ER. Once his patients left, they usually were gone for good.

For the first time, he felt a pang and realized he would miss Hickory Hollow when he went back.

The conversation shifted to a more introductory direction as his parents shared about their lives back in the city and Lena told about growing up here in town and eventually taking over her aunt's work.

"I'm sure Todd's told you how important family is to him," Mom said with what she probably thought was a sneaky look between them. His mom, the most obvious matchmaker in history. He'd have to let her down gently later tonight. "He's always been close with his grandfather," she added.

Todd felt another pang. Was that true? Grandfather never was shy about telling Todd the path he'd chosen for him or of being proud of Todd's accomplishments when he followed that path. But was that true closeness?

"Grandfather will be happy to see you at the reunion in two weeks," Dad said.

Todd had almost forgotten about the big family reunion in the daily busyness here. When the reunion arrived, his time in Hickory Hollow would be almost over.

"Do you think we can get David and Ruby to come? I want to talk to them about it this weekend," Mom said.

Todd shrugged.

"Your aunt Angela was hoping to convince Tyler to come," Dad said. "Maybe you could text him and encourage it."

Todd frowned. "I can try." But he doubted it would make a difference.

He saw Lena's confused expression.

"My grandfather cut ties with my cousin almost fifteen years ago." It had caused some drama in the family. Todd's parents and aunt and uncle had disagreed with Grandfather's decision to cut Tyler out of the will and refuse him admittance to family functions. Mom and Dad had stopped attending family events until Grandfather relented. But by then, Tyler had moved to another state and cut ties with the family.

Todd had been a sophomore in high school when Tyler was a sophomore in college. He'd seemed so worldly and sophisticated. Smart and proud.

Before the falling-out, Todd would've said Tyler was Grandfather's favorite grandkid. He'd been premed and top of his class.

Tyler had stopped communicating with the extended family for years after the blowout with Grandfather. It had only been in the past five years that Todd had reached out to him and they'd become friends.

Lena clearly didn't know what to say, and Todd realized he'd been lost in his thoughts.

"What do you think everyone would think of Lena?" Mom asked, breaking the awkward silence that had descended. Still matchmaking.

A pink blush rose in Lena's cheeks.

"I know what I think," Dad said. His eyes were twinkling. He was getting in on the act with Mom. "I like you. And I can see that my son does, too."

Chapter Thirteen

"It's not uncommon to experience nausea and vomiting in your third trimester," Lena said.

Her patient, Tamara Riehl, looked pale with a tinge of green as she reclined on the bed. But Lena scrawled her vitals on the paper chart at the counter. Everything was normal.

But Tamara was complaining of pain near her belly button and on her right side.

"Tamara only had morning sickness during the first few weeks with our older two boys."

Lena had been attempting to pretend that Tamara's husband, John, wasn't in the room.

It was silly, and it'd been more than a decade now. But a part of her still felt sixteen and left reeling from hearing him tell her that, even though they'd been on two buggy rides together on Sunday afternoons, he didn't want to see her again.

She was a professional. And even though *Aendi* Carol had been the one to birth Tamara's two other children, Lena could do this. She forced herself to put aside her personal feelings as she addressed them both. "Even so, each pregnancy can be different."

Tamara shifted on the bed and something in her expression pinched.

"A contraction?" Lena asked.

Tamara exhaled loudly through her nose. "It doesn't feel like a contraction."

"It's too early," John said. "There's two months to go."

Lena moved to the bed and put a gentle hand on Tamara's stomach. "Babies come in their own time."

But he was right. If Tamara was going into labor this early, it meant a high-risk delivery.

But Lena didn't think Tamara was in labor. With two small children at home, it was possible she'd overdone it and pulled a muscle, already stretched by the growing baby.

But she would rather err on the side of caution.

"If you'd like, I can phone over to the clinic and ask the doctor to stop by and check you over," she told Tamara.

John was already nodding before she'd finished speaking.

And some tension bled off Tamara. "Yes, that would be *goot*."

She excused herself and crossed the center to the telephone.

The call connected almost immediately, and she heard the muffled sound of Todd excusing himself. Had he left a patient midexam just to answer her call?

"Lena?"

Just hearing his voice, deep and confident, made her feel as if everything would be all right.

She cleared her throat, hoping that might mute the happiness she couldn't quite contain. "One of my patients is complaining of stomach pain. She's in her third trimester and I'm fairly confident she's not in labor. If you can spare the time, I'd appreciate if you could examine her."

"I've got to put stitches in the King boy, then I'll wrap up and head to you."

Before she could ask, he said, "Yes, stitches again," in a dry voice.

She couldn't stop the smile this time. He could probably hear it in her voice. "At least you've got the practice in."

"Ha."

They rang off, and she was just about to enter the exam room to let Tamara know when she heard her name from inside and paused behind the partially open door.

"I trust Lena," Tamara said. "This isn't labor. It's something else."

"I wish Carol were here," John said. "She delivered Daniel and Caleb."

"Lena apprenticed with her *aendi* for years," Tamara said. "And she pours all of herself into the center."

"I suppose she doesn't have much else to do, since she doesn't have a family of her own."

Lena fell back a step, her heart aching at his casual observation. She tried to take a deep breath, but the cut from hearing those words was deep and she was shocked by the sudden pain.

She doesn't have anything else.

She loved working for the center, helping her patients. This was her calling.

But his words had touched on her long-ago pain.

And after the useless meeting with Isaiah Speicher, she wondered how much longer she could keep the center open. The first letter from the director had threatened a shutdown if the center remained out of compliance.

The front door opened, shocking her from the swirl of hurt and thoughts. She stuck her head inside the room and let the couple know the doctor would arrive in a little while.

Ruby and her two girls waited inside the main room.

Lena settled Mindy and Maggie with a few toys she kept in a basket for just that purpose and brought Ruby into the second exam room.

She was distracted through the routine checkup. Thank goodness Ruby and the baby seemed healthy.

"How have you been feeling?" Lena asked as she stepped away from the bed in one of the center's rooms. She moved toward the counter and the chart she'd left there to record, tucking away her fetoscope as she went.

Ruby swatted at wrinkles on her dress and straightened her apron as she sat up.

"Some days I have so much energy that I can outlast the girls at their play, cook supper and still want to read a book before bed. And some days I'm so tired I can't remember whether I've done the most basic chores."

Lena had to smile at Ruby's description, so familiar to what she'd heard before from women in the second trimester.

"You look healthy, and the baby's heartbeat is strong." Ruby was showing now, just a hint of a baby bump.

Her hand curved over her stomach protectively. "We haven't told the girls yet."

Small voices murmured from the front room.

"No, I suppose not. Your news would be spread all over the county."

Both women shared a smile, though Lena's heart was heavy.

"They will be excited, I think," Ruby said with a fond look on her face. "To welcome a new brother or sister."

Lena nodded as she scrawled her notes onto paper. She heard the bed creak as Ruby stood up.

"Speaking of brothers, we heard you had dinner with Todd on Friday. And his parents."

Whatever pleasure Lena had felt after Friday evening's supper was muted now by the hurt she'd just experienced. She should've expected Ruby would bring it up.

Her *aendi* Kate had, when Lena had seen her at house church that same weekend.

"Be careful you don't get too attached," *Aendi* Kate had cautioned her.

Lena had felt only a nip of embarrassment, too busy reliving the joyful moments of the interaction between Todd and his parents, the obvious love they shared. The gentle teasing that went both ways. Kimberly and Michael had made her feel like she belonged.

Since it had grown dark while they'd visited over after-dinner coffees, Todd had driven her home. He'd been relaxed and talkative, telling more stories about his childhood and his family.

Now all she could think of was how little time they had left. Less than three weeks.

He wasn't staying.

"We're only friends." She couldn't help the cool bite to her words, the wound fresh in her heart. "Nothing more."

Movement from the doorway drew Ruby's gaze first, then Lena's.

Todd.

Had he overheard her? It was difficult to tell from the grim set of his lips.

Her hurt was so fresh that she needed a moment to gather herself.

She couldn't quite meet Ruby's concerned gaze. "Do you have any more questions?"

Ruby replied in the negative and Lena excused herself.

"Let me wash up," she said as she passed Todd in the doorway. "Then we can see Tamara and John."

She ducked into the washroom and ran water from the faucet. She pressed cold, trembling fingers to her eyes.

She had to go out there and be professional. Tamara needed care.

And nothing was going to change with Todd, even if her own feelings had grown unwieldy.

It didn't matter if she prayed for Todd every night. For a way for things to change, so that they might be together.

They were from two different worlds. She would never fit into his city life, nor could she leave her duties here.

Wishing for more was hopeless.

Todd followed Lena down the hall to the exam room a few minutes later.

He'd said goodbye to Ruby and been covered with hugs and kisses from Mindy and Maggie before they'd left in the buggy Ruby drove.

Something was wrong with Lena.

We're only friends. Nothing more.

He'd never heard the cool, almost snappish tone from her before. She wouldn't meet his gaze as she'd brushed past him and ducked into the restroom, and when she'd emerged, her eyes had been red rimmed.

All signs that pointed to something wrong.

But now wasn't the time to find out what it was. Lena had called him because she had a patient who needed an exam.

He shook hands with Tamara and John as Lena made introductions.

Lena handed him a clipboard with her charts that held records of vital signs and Lena's careful notes through the seven-month pregnancy.

He had grown to love how detailed Lena's charts were and looked up from the clipboard, a smile blooming—but she cut her eyes away.

Right. Focus.

"Tamara and John have two other children," Lena said. "Their older son is five and their second is three."

"Were there any complications with either of those pregnancies?" He meant the question for Lena, but included husband and wife with a glance.

"No." Lena was the one who answered.

"I've felt fine, just like before," Tamara said. "Until a few days ago."

Todd handed the chart to Lena and took his stethoscope out of his pocket. He stepped to the side of the bed.

"You had that heartburn at the beginning," John reminded his wife gently.

Tamara shrugged. "Only for a few days."

"Mind if I listen to your lungs and heart?" Todd held up the silver end of the stethoscope.

Tamara shook her head. "Go ahead."

"What happened a few days ago?" Todd asked after he'd taken a few moments with the stethoscope. Tamara's heart and lungs sounded normal.

"I felt queasy after lunch and couldn't keep my dinner down." Her eyebrows pinched. "I thought perhaps I'd caught something from one of the children, but neither of them have been sick."

"Her appetite has been off, and she seems more tired than usual," John offered.

It sounded like a common virus. Tamara's vitals were good. She wasn't flushed with fever.

When he glanced up to get Lena's take, she had her arms wrapped around her middle and was staring off into the distance out the window. He had never seen her so distracted when in the room with a patient before.

Was it *these* patients? Was there a reason she was holding herself aloof?

Or was it him?

"And you're having abdominal pain?" he asked Tamara.

She nodded, then blushed. "I don't know…it could be gas." She whispered the last.

He laughed a little. "Don't be ashamed of that. Your body is doing amazing work taking care of that little one."

After a short conference in the hall with Lena, they sent the couple home, advising them that it could be a common virus, but to come to the clinic or back to the center if symptoms worsened or Tamara developed a fever.

"Thank you for coming," Lena said.

Had she meant the words as a dismissal? Because she left him in the hallway and went into the exam room where she stripped the top sheet from the bed and put away the implements she'd used.

He stepped into the room, blocking the door.

"I sent away the handful of patients waiting to see me at the clinic, told them to come back tomorrow. Do you want to grab some dinner?"

She ran water from the faucet and began scrubbing the counter. All without looking at him. "I can't today. I need to clean up and then do some weeding in my garden."

Weeding the garden. Was that an excuse? It seemed like an excuse.

What's wrong?

For some reason, the words stuck in his throat. She'd dismissed what was growing between them.

We're only friends. Nothing more.

He'd thought it was more. Friday night, she'd fallen so easily into a camaraderie with his parents. They'd sat in his car in her driveway for a half hour after he'd parked.

She kept popping into his thoughts at all

hours—the way she'd turned her head on the headrest so that their eyes met; the shy smile that slayed him; the way the starlight had cast silver gleams on her hair and her face.

He'd wanted to kiss her. Badly.

But the last time they'd been close enough to kiss, she'd pulled away.

And he didn't want to mess things up between them.

Except maybe he already had. He wracked his brain, trying to think of what he might've said to offend her. Or maybe something had happened before he'd arrived.

He wanted to comfort her. At the same time, he was afraid of saying the wrong thing.

He watched her in silence for a few more moments before speaking. "Do you ever want more than this?"

He didn't even know what he was really asking.

Maybe did she want more than living alone and working day and night at the clinic? Or maybe did she want more than friendship? More from him?

She scrubbed particularly hard at a spot on the counter. "The center is all I have," she said, so quietly he almost couldn't hear her with her shoulder turned like it was. "Why would I ever think about leaving it?"

Other words gathered in his chest, making him ache. *You have me*.

She stopped scrubbing and sighed, still not looking at him. "I have more work to do. I'll see you later."

There was no question this time. Her words were a clear dismissal.

There was nothing more for him to do except leave.

Emotion rolled through him in a tsunami, and a sudden spike of anger made him turn his car back toward the city.

If Lena didn't want his friendship, what was he doing here?

He only got ten minutes down the road when he began to cool off and reason returned.

He'd promised his brother he was staying for the full six weeks. He had patients coming to the clinic tomorrow. He couldn't let them down.

He didn't know what had happened with Lena, but this wasn't the end for them. If she wanted to be alone this evening, so be it. That didn't stop him from praying for her, praying that whatever hurt she faced would be taken from her.

And maybe he would call on her in the morning. Bring donuts.

He couldn't leave things like this.

Chapter Fourteen

Todd couldn't say when the nudge inside him started, but it got louder and louder as the day went on.

Until something inside was shouting for him to check on Tamara Riehl.

He wrapped up with the last patient of the day at the clinic and as the older man left through the front door, Todd went to the desk, where Mrs. Smith was organizing paperwork for tomorrow's patients.

"Do we have a file on Tamara Riehl? Or her husband, John? They have two small children." He couldn't remember the names, though Tamara had mentioned them yesterday.

"I can look."

He and Mrs. Smith weren't bosom buddies, not the way he and Lena were—or had been up until yesterday. Lena would've registered the urgency in him.

"Can you do it now?" he prodded when Mrs. Smith didn't get up from the desk. He knew Doc Bradshaw's records weren't digitized. Whatever file there was would be in the massive file cabinets in the doc's old office.

"Okay."

But Mrs. Smith seemed to move like molasses.

Since he'd asked her to complete this new task, Todd busied himself cleaning up the exam room he'd just used to save his office manager from having to do it.

She met him in the hallway as he was leaving the exam room. "We do have a file."

She handed him a file folder and he thanked her and dismissed her for the day.

He wasted no time. Of course there was no phone number listed in the patient information. Only an address.

Todd's urgency grew as he locked up the clinic and went to his car, checking that his medical bag was in the trunk.

He tried to tell himself that he was being ridiculous. Yesterday, he'd told the Riehls to come to the clinic if Tamara's symptoms worsened, and they hadn't come.

That meant she was fine, didn't it?

But the feeling of unease wouldn't leave him.

He entered the address into the GPS built into his car. It would only take ten minutes to go to their house, check on Tamara. He'd be back to his rented room in less than half an hour.

When he was on the road, he wished Lena was beside him. She would've known where the Riehls lived without having to dig for an address. She knew where everyone lived. Or at least that's what it seemed like.

She would've told him to stop being silly. That everything was fine.

Or maybe she wouldn't. Maybe she would've told him to trust his gut.

He hoped he wasn't about to make a fool of himself.

When he arrived at the address he'd input, he saw a neat little farm with a couple of cows in the field. Dark pants and colorful shirts and dresses hung on clotheslines beside the house, flying in the breeze like lively flags.

He left his bag in the car. This wasn't a house call. Not really.

When he knocked on the door, an unfamiliar Amish woman answered.

"Hello, I'm Doctor Barrett. From the clinic."

A little boy in dark pants and a red shirt ran up behind the woman and hid his face in her skirts.

"Is this the home of Tamara Riehl?"

"That's *Mamm*!" the little boy said, peeking up at Todd.

So he at least had the right address. What was he supposed to say now? He'd come all the way out here because of a bad feeling?

"Is Tamara home? Or John?"

The woman finally spoke. "John's there." She pointed and he turned to see John walking across the field toward them. His pants and boots were dusty, like he'd been working hard at his farming—whatever that entailed. Todd didn't know what kind of a farmer he was.

A few moments passed while Todd waited. When John joined him on the porch, the man seemed unperturbed and maybe a little confused to see him.

"I want to check on Tamara," Todd explained. He didn't mention his gut or that feeling.

John led the way into the house.

There was a chorus of "*Daeds*" from two little boy voices, and John accepted hugs to his legs and then patted their heads and sent them into the kitchen.

"She was fine earlier," the woman said. "She laid down for a nap."

Todd still hadn't been given her name.

"My sister," John introduced. "She's been helping some with the boys. I'll go wake Tamara. It'll be dinner soon anyway and hopefully she'll want to eat."

John walked down a short hallway, and Todd was left to admire the colorful handwoven rug and simple furnishings in the living room. John's sister had gone into the kitchen and Todd heard a clank of pots and pans. The two little boys hung back in the kitchen doorway, sneaking peeks at him.

"Doc!" came John's shout from a room at the back of the house. "Come quick!"

Todd didn't hesitate. He rushed down the hallway to the door standing open.

Afternoon sunlight illuminated the room through an open window. Tamara lay in the bed, her face flushed with fever. John was at her side, hovering over the edge of the bed.

"My stomach," she moaned. She had one hand pressed lower than the baby.

"She was sleeping, but restless. Moving her legs when I came in the room," John said. "She was fine earlier."

Todd could hear the worry in the man's voice. "Can you get my medical bag from the car?"

Todd touched Tamara's forehead briefly as John left the room. She was burning up.

"When did your fever start?"

"I don't—know," she gasped. "I started getting chills after I laid down, I guess."

"It's not labor pains?" He knew it wasn't. Not when she was pressing her right hand low on her belly on that side.

"Doesn't feel like it did with the other ones," she mumbled. She turned her head on the pillow, moaning low.

He met John in the hallway. "She needs a hospital."

John's eyes were already wide and frightened. "Is it the baby?"

"I think it could be appendicitis."

John shook his head. "What's that?"

"It's an inflammation or infection of the appendix. I can't know for sure without doing some tests. Maybe an ultrasound. I can't do any of those things here. Or at the clinic." He spoke before John could even make the suggestion.

"If her appendix ruptures, she could die. The baby, too. I want to call an ambulance."

John seemed to understand the gravity of the situation. "All right."

Todd made the call from his cell phone, taking her vitals as he did. Her blood pressure was high, same with her temperature.

"When was the last time you felt the baby move?" he asked.

"I—I don't know." She was gritting her teeth through the pain, and tears were falling from her eyes.

It seemed forever until the ambulance arrived and took Tamara and John. Todd promised to call the hospital to check on them.

John's sister stayed with the boys, and Todd drove without conscious thought to what he was doing.

It shouldn't have been a surprise that he ended up in front of Lena's center. The parking area was empty. He didn't even know whether she was home.

He sat in his car, clutching the steering wheel for a long time.

Why had he come? He'd followed his heart here. His heart wanted Lena.

Yesterday, she'd made it clear she hadn't wanted to see him. He couldn't muster the will to get out of the car, afraid she'd send him away again.

He just needed…

He needed…

The front door opened and she appeared.

* * *

Lena stood on the threshold and watched as Todd got out of his car.

She'd been making the bed in the room that faced the road and seen him drive up. She didn't know why he'd come, but she'd gotten worried when he sat in his car for so long.

He looked haggard, his face pale. Almost shell-shocked.

It was enough to send her off the step and toward him. "What happened?"

"I just left Tamara and John's. I sent them to the hospital."

Oh no.

"Is she all right?"

He shook his head. No? Or he didn't know? "I suspect appendicitis. I should've sent her on to the hospital yesterday—"

She crossed to him. It didn't matter that he didn't move toward her. Only that he was upset and he'd come here. To her.

At the last moment, he reached for her. She moved into his embrace easily.

Oh.

It felt like coming home.

The tangy scent of his soap where her nose pressed into his neck.

The flex of muscle in his shoulder beneath her cheek.

The strength of his arms as they held her close.

She closed her eyes against the raw emotion that made her throat burn.

In this moment, her feelings didn't matter. Only Todd did.

Her arms went around his waist and her hands pressed against his back. Holding him just as he was holding her.

She'd never hugged anyone like this. Not even her *daed.*

Todd's jaw rested against the crown of her head. He inhaled, and she felt some of his tension leave on a shuddery sigh.

She didn't want anything to break the magic of this moment, but she also wondered whether talking about it would help.

"Did Tamara come to the clinic?" she finally asked.

She heard the rumble of Todd's voice in his chest before the words emerged. "No. No, it was the strangest thing…"

He laughed a little, his arms tightening about her minutely. "I couldn't stop thinking about her. All day long while I saw other patients, something about the exam yesterday plagued me. So I got the address from Mrs. Smith and went on an unofficial house call."

He told her about the symptoms he'd observed, about John hiding his fear while they waited for the ambulance. About the little boys watching wide-eyed from the kitchen as the paramedics wheeled Tamara out of the house.

As he spoke, his tension ratcheted higher and higher.

"Come in for some tea," she said, pushing away, hoping to break him from the tension of the moment.

"Tea cures all ills?" He said the teasing words but his expression was bleak.

"Something like that."

He followed her inside.

Dusk had fallen around them and walking inside, where she had battery-powered lamps lit, was a shock to her senses.

She put on the kettle and before she could urge Todd to sit at the table, he'd paced away into the kitchen nook. He had his cell phone out and was tapping on the screen.

When he caught her looking, he motioned with his index finger in the air. He lifted the phone to his ear.

He was calling the hospital, she realized as he identified himself. He was only on the call for a minute or so before he rang off.

He shoved his phone in his pocket, his shoulders slumped. He ran one hand down his face, weariness and frustration evident in his grim expression.

"Appendicitis," he confirmed. "They're taking Tamara into surgery."

Oh no.

Suddenly feeling weak, she leaned back against the counter. "What about the baby? Isn't a surgery this late in pregnancy risky?"

He gripped the back of his neck. "Surgery always has risks. But if her appendix ruptures, both of them could die."

She closed her eyes. Was there anything she could have noticed when Tamara had been in the clinic? Everything the woman had mentioned could have been a normal part of pregnancy. Couldn't it?

"I should've known yesterday," he said. He sounded angry and defeated.

How could he blame himself?

"If there'd been a hospital closer, I wouldn't have hesitated to send her for more tests. Someone would've picked it up twenty-four hours ago."

She put tea bags in two mugs.

She moved closer to him, a few feet away, her hand on the back of one of the kitchen chairs. "And if the doctor or ultrasound tech or whoever missed the diagnosis?" she asked. "Would you still be blaming yourself?"

"I don't know."

Looking at him, she saw the vulnerability that he didn't show to anyone else.

It was as if sharing that first embrace had dropped the walls between them. This time it was easier to cross the three steps between them and reach for him.

She hugged him this time, her arms around his middle. His hands clasped behind her lower back.

"What changed?" he whispered into her ear, his head ducked low. "Yesterday, you wouldn't even talk to me."

She'd been acting foolish. Like a silly teenager, brokenhearted because she'd been rejected by the boy she'd liked.

Seeing Todd tonight, outside, so disheartened and vulnerable, had made her realize that as much as she needed him, he needed her, too.

Maybe their friendship wouldn't last after he went back to Columbus.

Maybe she did only have the center.

But Todd was here now. And as much as it might hurt later, she couldn't just walk away from the friendship she'd grown to depend on. To cherish.

"Lena?" he whispered.

She'd been so lost in her thoughts she hadn't answered him.

She couldn't tell him about John's years-ago rejection, or the words that had hurt her so badly.

But she did say, "I don't want to lose your friendship."

He leaned back slightly, one of his hands moving to curl around her jaw. Butterflies took flight inside her at the intimate touch. His eyes searched her face.

"Is that all we have? Friendship?"

He leaned in and brushed her lips with a kiss. The sweet, fluttering butterflies turned into a maelstrom.

Her lashes fluttered and then she was staring at him with wide eyes as he brushed her nose with his. Once, then again.

He smiled a crooked smile. "It feels like more to me."

There was a fraction of a second where she could've pulled away. But she didn't.

She met his kiss eagerly, her heart pounding in her ears.

His thumb brushed her cheek as his lips slanted over hers. Her eyes drifted closed.

Todd was kissing her.

The teakettle shrieked, and they both jumped.

She whirled away, snatching the teakettle from the stove with shaking hands.

They shouldn't have done that. She shouldn't have let him kiss her.

Or, if she was honest with herself, she shouldn't have kissed him back.

But it hadn't felt wrong.

It had felt like the first true thing she'd admitted to herself since he'd arrived on her doorstep.

Chapter Fifteen

⟡

"I kissed her," Todd blurted.

David dropped the leather strap he was holding and stared.

Todd held the horse's halter as David unhitched the animal from the buggy.

It was Saturday morning, and when Todd had arrived at David's for a visit, his brother had come out of the house with a daughter in each arm. He'd declared that Ruby needed some quiet time and that he wanted to take the girls for a buggy ride.

Todd had surprised him by offering to drive. They'd spent a pleasant hour toodling around the countryside in David's enclosed buggy, the girls chattering about everything and nothing.

The driving surprise had nothing on this one.

David's eyebrows nearly reached his hat.

Todd hadn't meant to blurt out the words, but there they were. "I kissed Lena," he admitted, just in case there was any confusion who they were talking about.

David cleared his throat. "I heard you." He went back to unbuckling the leather harness.

Todd couldn't stop thinking about the kiss. It was easier thinking about that than how he'd almost lost a patient. He'd spoken to Tamara's surgeon late last night and again this morning.

She'd come through the surgery but the trauma had sent her into early labor. They'd done an emergency C-section to save the baby. A little girl.

The baby was in the NICU and Tamara was still recovering.

And Todd couldn't help thinking that maybe things could've been different if he'd sent Tamara to the hospital on Thursday.

The kiss with Lena was the distraction he needed. She'd been so sweet. Having her in his arms had been right.

She'd pushed the teacup into his hands, and he'd taken it to humor her, even though he wasn't a tea kind of guy.

They'd sat at the table talking for a long time. She'd distracted him with questions about growing up with Henry, his school days, stories from her own childhood.

He hadn't kissed her good-night, though he'd wanted to. Well, he'd kissed her cheek when he'd taken his leave. But that didn't count.

David finished what he was doing with the harness, and it released from the horse. The animal took a step forward, and Todd would've been knocked over if he hadn't sidestepped.

He still had hold of the harness and gave a gentle tug. "Whoa."

Remarkably, the horse stopped. The big animal blew out a puff of hot, smelly air that hit right in Todd's face and made his nose wrinkle.

"You're getting better with him," David said.

During those first weeks of getting to know his adult brother, Todd had been wary of the animal that was big enough to break his foot with a well-placed hoof.

"I guess he isn't so bad," Todd said.

"It's a *goot* thing. Being able to drive a buggy. Getting more comfortable with the horse." David paused. "When you join the Amish church, you won't be able to drive your fancy car."

Whoa. What?

"What are you talking about?"

David sent a glance to the house. Mindy was

supervising Maggie as they dug in the mud in the garden near the back door. Both girls were fine.

Then David looked back at Todd. His expression was serious. "Lena joined the church when she was seventeen or eighteen. Most Amish women do. It isn't something she decided on a whim. She dedicated her life to the church and our community here."

He knew that. "What are you saying?"

"She isn't going to leave."

There was a finality to the words. It reverberated through Todd. All of a sudden, he felt off-kilter.

"I didn't ask her to leave."

David kept staring at him with that solemn gaze. "Are you going to join the Amish church? Move here permanently?"

Todd had never thought of it. For a moment, he imagined what it would be like. Living near the clinic. A landline the most technology he used in any one day. Walking or riding a bike or driving a buggy to get around.

The simplicity of it. The slow pace. Being a part of the close-knit community.

But he shook his head. "You know I can't. I have commitments." Grandfather had been unhappy with Todd delaying joining the ER.

"You aren't a part of this family anymore."

The words rang through Todd's memory. He wasn't supposed to have overheard the conversation between Grandfather and Tyler. He'd been passing through the hallway in his grandparents' massive house and stopped cold outside Grandfather's office. Grandfather had been behind the desk, out of sight, but Todd had a clear view of Tyler. And the expression of devastation that he wore.

Grandfather had funded Todd's medical school costs. Todd had an expectation to fulfill.

And there was a part of Todd that was still frightened and frustrated by what had happened with Tamara. She could've died. Her baby was facing weeks in the NICU and she would have a long recovery.

Todd couldn't even think about what might've happened if he hadn't gone out on that house call. If he'd gone home from the clinic and turned off his phone, would John have taken her to the hospital on his own? Or back to Lena's, when every minute counted?

One of Todd's future colleagues had been the one to save Tamara and her baby.

"The work I do in Columbus is important," he said.

David nodded. "And the work that Lena does is important."

Of course it was. He'd seen it firsthand. David was saying that Lena was too enmeshed here. Too much a part of the community to leave it.

But while Todd had been dropped into her life and experienced it, she'd never been a part of his.

How could David say Lena wouldn't like being a part of Todd's city life, when neither of them knew?

Dad had reminded him about the family reunion. It would be the perfect chance for Lena to meet his family. Once she met Grandfather, she'd understand the legacy Todd had to carry. He could take her to see his apartment. To the hospital.

He was falling for her. And he knew she had feelings for him, too. Maybe there was a chance she'd be happy moving to the city.

Maybe she would choose him.

"Be careful with her heart," David said finally.

"What about my heart?" Todd joked.

David didn't answer. Maybe he didn't get it.

There was a fine tension between them, one that hadn't been there before. Until now, they'd always been careful around each other. They watched what they said. They'd still been getting to know each other.

But David hadn't pulled his punches today. Maybe it was because Lena was part of the Amish community.

And Todd wasn't.

The morning sun was just rising over the horizon as Lena lifted one of the clean, damp sheets from a deep basket and lifted it to hang over the clothesline.

It had been a few days since the kiss and she still couldn't stop thinking about it. About Todd.

They'd delivered another baby together last night around nine. *Mamm* and *boppli* were inside sleeping—she'd peeked in to the room only a bit ago before she'd come out here to hang the clean linens.

Last night, Todd had been professional and focused. Even more so than the first night, the first *boppli*. It wasn't that he was stressed or frustrated. It was more of an alertness. As if he didn't want to miss the tiniest sign that something might be wrong.

Was his extra vigilance because of what had happened with Tamara? It had to be.

Maybe once Tamara and her little girl came home and Todd saw that they were all right, he'd be able to relax.

Or would he even be in Hickory Hollow when that happened?

She was aware of their time together ticking down like the hands of a clock. Todd had to return to the city in less than three weeks.

Every time she thought about it, her insides twisted. She tried to keep her focus elsewhere, but it popped into her brain at all hours.

The quiet sound of his car drew her attention. Bright headlights cut across the yard and illuminated her for a second.

She was still blinking against the halo of light in her eyes when she heard his car door close and the crunch of his shoes on the gravel as he approached.

"You're up early." His voice was quiet, like the morning around them. "Everything okay?"

"So are you. Mama and *boppli* are fine. They were stable overnight and are asleep."

In the growing light, she saw his eyes flick toward the center and back to her. She bent to lift the next sheet from the basket and straightened to drape it across the line.

Todd had followed her, standing opposite on the other side of the line. The damp sheet was between them and when she moved to clip a wooden clothespin on the line, Todd's hand closed over hers.

She raised her brows. Lifted her left hand to place a clip there.

He gently clasped that hand, too, so both hands were connected. They stood with the line and sheet between them.

His eyes were warm. "Hi."

Her stomach dipped at the husky tone in his voice. "Hi."

"You might've noticed I didn't kiss you good-night." Where he clasped her right hand, he threaded their fingers together.

The touch became more intimate, though it was just their fingers tangled together. Warmth bloomed in her middle and radiated outward.

"It barely registered." Was that her voice, breathless and husky?

Something lit in his eyes—pleasure?—that she'd teased him. One corner of his mouth crooked up. "I'm not surprised your brain was already five steps ahead, anticipating what Mom or Baby needed next. You were amazing last night. You always are."

His compliment warmed her even more than his touch. "I was only doing my job."

He threaded the fingers of their other hands together. "I know. That's what makes you so amazing. And I really wanted to kiss you last night."

She hadn't realized. She'd walked him to the door—maybe he was right, her mind had already been counting off the next several things she needed to do—and he'd hugged her briefly before he'd gone. She'd spent a few seconds standing on the inside of the closed door, already missing him.

"Why didn't you?" She could only whisper the words that made her vulnerable.

"David lectured me." He said the words sheepishly.

She was surprised. He'd told his brother?

"I don't want either of us to have a broken heart when I go back to Columbus."

She was becoming afraid it was too late for that. She was under no illusions that he would stay. When he went, she would miss him. She would never be the same.

His thumb gently rubbed over the knuckles of her left hand. He was waiting for her to say something.

She lifted her chin minutely. "I promise not to have a broken heart if you won't."

His eyes smiled at her first, before the expression broke over his face like the sun rising. "Promise."

He glanced behind her, to the house. The windows were still dark.

When he looked back at her, his eyes were lit from within. "If I could be sure our new mama wasn't watching through the window, I'd kiss you right now."

The first-time mother probably was still asleep. She had to be exhausted after laboring much of the day yesterday and waking up in the night to feed the baby.

But there was a small chance that she was awake. And that was enough.

Todd might've spoken to David, but Lena didn't want anyone else knowing her business. These moments were for her and Todd alone.

"Maybe we can see each other soon. Outside of work." He couldn't know how hard the words were for her to say, as awkward and roundabout as they were.

His warm smile reassured her. "I was hoping you felt that way."

He was?

Some of the uncertainty fled.

"Do you remember my dad mentioning the family reunion? It's this weekend, in the city. Would you come with me?"

She hadn't been expecting that. Other than David, Todd's family was made up of *Englishers*. She would be an oddity. And they weren't even a couple—not really.

He must've sensed her hesitation. "Only if you don't have any patients who will need you."

Oh. He thought she was hesitating because of her duties here.

"I would love to spend the time with you—"

"Good."

"—but I don't want to distract you from being with your family." She knew how important those relationships were to him. "Will Henry be there?"

"I don't know. And you won't be a distraction. My family will love you. My mom is still asking when she can visit with you again."

"All right. I'll go with you."

His face lit up and she pushed away her concerns. She wanted this time with Todd. And even though his family would be present, it was a chance for them to spend time together where she didn't have to constantly look over her shoulder and wonder who was watching her and whether word would get back to her *mamm* or *Aendi* Kate.

Todd squeezed her hands and finally let her go. She felt bereft without his touch. But she had laundry to finish.

And his attention had shifted to the center. She recognized the professional mask that had slipped over his demeanor.

"You can go in," she said as she lifted the next clean sheet. "I'll only be a couple of minutes behind you. The *boppli* will wake up hungry any minute."

"Can I bring over some lunch later?"

"You don't have to. I'm sure relatives will want to visit the new baby." She meant to caution him that they wouldn't have any time alone.

But his smile didn't slip. "That's all right. I only have to be in the same room with you to make the trip worth it."

She didn't get those words out of her mind all day long.

Chapter Sixteen

"So you're a nurse?"

Lena shook her head at the curious question from one of Todd's distant cousins.

"She's a midwife. It's not the same," Todd said from his place beside her. He launched into an explanation of what she did at the center, but Lena tuned out.

Todd's extended family was huge. Aunts, uncles, cousins, second cousins. Even a great-grandmother was here somewhere. The family had rented a pavilion in a wide grassy area at one of the beautiful lakes within easy driving distance of the city. It was sunny and a pleasant breeze stirred her skirts.

Todd's hand rested at her lower back. It wasn't a casual touch. More of a claim. She was here with him, and he'd stuck by her side all morning.

Todd's family was gracious and kind. She'd been introduced to so many cousins and aunts and uncles that she'd never be able to keep them all straight. No one had stared at her *kapp* or her simple dress. Either Todd's mother had warned them all that Lena would be here today, or they'd had some introduction to the Amish from David and Ruby.

Lena had been disappointed to learn that David and Ruby wouldn't be here today, but the couple had a commitment at home to attend to.

"Is that—" Todd's cousin—Lena had already forgotten his name—asked the question.

Raised excited voices drifted over from the sidewalk that connected the pavilion to the parking area. She couldn't see what or who the Barrett family was gathering around.

"It's Tyler." Todd sounded shocked. His hand fell away and Lena felt a tiny pang at the loss of his touch. "Do you mind—"

He glanced down at her, already on the balls of his feet, itching to follow his cousin and talk to Tyler. He'd shared with her about Tyler's troubles with the family patriarch.

But there was also a warm, steady light in Todd's eyes that was for Lena alone.

Her stomach tipped. "Go," she said with a little push to his arm. "I'll stay here."

He jogged off, and she watched as the crowd parted, saw him embrace another man with dark hair and a chiseled jaw like Todd's.

Lena moved away to a cement picnic table that had been draped with a colorful paper covering. Beyond it, the lake was peaceful and blue, the sun glinting off its surface.

What was she doing here? With a little distance from Todd, she recognized that her feelings were tangled in knots. Being here with him today had blurred the lines in their relationship.

She liked the way he claimed her just by standing next to her, the turn of his shoulders that showed everyone she was here with him.

She liked every touch. The brush of his hand on hers as he'd helped her out of the car, the touch at her shoulder when he'd pointed out something across the park, the purposeful bump of his shoulder against hers while they'd stood in line to get lunch earlier.

She liked Todd. More than that. She was falling for him.

And she still couldn't see a future for them. She'd prayed nonstop since their first kiss. For a clear answer. For a way they could be together.

She couldn't see how it could work.

But she also couldn't help how she felt. No one had ever made her feel the way Todd did.

She didn't want to lose him.

"You look pensive. Have we worn you out?" Kimberly's voice called out from a few steps away.

Lena looked up and realized she'd been lost in her thoughts. She'd missed Todd's mother as she'd approached. Lena had to do a double take because the man just behind her could've been Todd's younger doppelgänger.

This must be Henry.

"I'm having a lovely time," Lena answered the question Kimberly had asked moments ago. "Just taking a moment to breathe."

Kimberly made introductions. Lena couldn't help but notice Henry's eyes narrow slightly as he took her in. The clasp of his hand as he shook hers was almost as curt as his smile.

"Todd mentioned you're a builder," she said. "Do you have a specialty?"

"I'm a general contractor." He didn't offer more than that. It left an awkward pause in the conversation.

Kimberly must have felt it, too. She exhaled through her nose before smiling at Lena. "Did Todd go in search of coffee?"

"He saw Tyler arrive and went to say hi."

"Oh, Tyler! I haven't seen that boy in years. Henry, would you stay and keep Lena company?" Kimberly was off without waiting for an answer.

And Lena was left with Todd's brother, who hadn't smiled once.

"I hope you'll have time for a conversation with Todd," she said. "He's been trying to reach you."

Some emotion she couldn't name glittered in Henry's eyes. "I'm surprised he came today."

"Why?"

"He's been spending so much time in Hickory Hollow. With David." He tipped his head. "And I guess, with you."

Was Henry jealous of Todd's connection with David? Why bring it up unless that was true?

"Todd and David have grown close, but that doesn't mean there's not room in Todd's life for you."

Henry exhaled a puff of air. He stared out over the water, giving her his profile. "Look… my brother's been playing small-town doctor, but we both know he isn't going to end up in Hickory Hollow. Has he even seen Grandfather today?"

She didn't know.

Henry's smile bloomed, but it was twisted. "Todd has always been under Grandfather's thumb. The old man let him have his little diversion, but as soon as Grandfather says 'go,' Todd will report to his real job in Columbus. He's not going to go against the old man's wishes."

Henry's words hit a soft spot that Lena didn't even know she had. She'd known all this time that Todd wasn't going to stay. But...was there a tiny, hidden part of her that had wanted to believe he would stay? That he would choose a simple life, a life that included her?

She must've had some kernel of hope, because at Henry's harsh words, it withered and died.

"I'm sorry," he said gruffly.

She smiled wanly and stared at the waves lapping at the shore. "You haven't said anything I don't already know."

Henry shifted his feet. Maybe he did have a heart after all. It was just buried beneath his tough exterior.

"Why don't you come to visit David?" she asked.

He breathed a laugh. "That's kinda personal."

She finally looked over at him. He was appraising her with an open frankness.

"You gave me some pretty personal advice," she said. "So...why don't you?"

He smiled a real smile this time. "I can see why Todd likes you."

His words made her blush. He changed the subject and it wasn't until later that she realized he'd never answered the question.

"I can't believe how big Amelia is," Todd said.

Tyler's little girl was playing tag with some other distant cousins in the open grass nearby.

The wave of family members who wanted to greet Tyler had dissipated and he and Todd had moved away to a little grassy knoll. Mom was chatting with Tyler's wife, Darci.

And a quick look told Todd that Lena was being entertained by… Henry? Sure enough, Todd's brother was chatting with her. Henry looked more relaxed than Todd could remember seeing him in recent memory. Good.

"How do you like Lakeview?" Tyler asked. "Are you making friends with the nurses?"

Todd shook his head. "I delayed my start date." He hadn't spoken to his cousin in a couple of months—since before he'd made the decision. He told Tyler about it, about adjusting to life in a small town, about delivering babies, about working with Lena.

"Ah. And that's Lena." Tyler nodded to where she still stood with Henry. He turned a sly smile on Todd. "You can't keep your eyes off her."

Heat crawled up Todd's neck. "She's…special."

Tyler's gaze cut to his wife, who was crouched in front of Amelia, looking at something in the girl's palm. "I get that." His focus returned to Todd. "What does Grandfather think about all of it?"

Trust Tyler to cut straight to the point.

Todd sighed. "I haven't seen him yet today. But last time we spoke, he wasn't happy about me pushing back my start date."

Tyler pushed his hands into the pockets of his jeans. "I can't imagine he's going to be happy to hear you plan to move to a small town to practice."

Todd found himself gaping at his cousin. He quickly recovered. "I'm not planning that."

He could still hear echoes of Grandfather yelling at Tyler from all those years ago. *You're not my grandson anymore!*

Tyler's brows crunched together. "You're— but the way you were just talking, I thought you wanted to stay."

"It's temporary."

"The way you were talking…"

What? Todd didn't ask the question, though

he was curious as to what his cousin thought he'd heard. Living in Hickory Hollow had been a change, and maybe there were things that Todd had learned. Like how to stop being such a slave to his technology. How to slow down and connect with the people who mattered.

But he couldn't stay.

"Grandfather has paved the way for this job for me." He couldn't say why his voice was rough when he said those words. "He connected me with the right people, in college, med school…" He'd basically gotten Todd the ER placement.

Tyler nodded. His eyes had gone a little squinty as he watched his wife and daughter.

"Do you ever…wish things had been different?" Todd asked.

"What, with Grandfather?" Tyler shook his head. His expression was relaxed, happy. "Darci was the best thing ever to happen to me. I recognized it back then and it's still true today. If I would've let Grandfather run my life, Darci and I wouldn't be together. I wouldn't have Amelia." Tyler shrugged. "So what if I didn't follow the family career path? I'm happy. More than happy."

Amelia ran up to her dad, interrupting their conversation. Tyler scooped her up, and Todd excused himself as his cousin's attention was diverted by Amelia telling him all about the flower she'd found.

Todd made his way toward Lena, who was chatting with Mom. Henry had disappeared.

Tyler was happy. But Todd still felt the weight of all the expectations that had been placed on him for the past decade.

He'd never bucked them. Not once. Never even thought of taking another path.

But Tyler's curious questions had set him spinning. Grandfather would be furious if Todd declined the ER job. It might fracture the family forever.

"Hey." Lena's hand slipped into his, her eyes searching his face.

His wayward thoughts had carried him all the way to her side without a conscious thought. It's where he wanted to be anyway.

"Your grandfather was looking for you," Mom said quietly. She wore a secretive smile.

Todd's feelings for Lena weren't a well-kept secret. He cleared his throat. "I need to talk to him, too. See if he has a connection in the department of health."

"I can wait here," Lena said as Mom slipped away.

Todd shook his head. "Come with me." Maybe

if Grandfather met her, he'd understand why Todd's head was in such a muddle. Lena was special. He'd said it to Tyler, and he was proud to have her by his side today.

They found Grandfather in the shade under the pavilion, sipping iced tea.

Grandfather's eyes were sharp behind his glasses, and he didn't miss Todd and Lena's clasped hands. Todd felt like he was back in middle school but resisted the urge to drop her hand like he was in trouble. He was a grown man.

"Grandfather, this is Lena." He went on to explain the work Lena did in her community, how she helped the mothers and babies.

Todd stalled out. The stubborn set to Grandfather's jaw was unmistakable.

"Todd has been a big help to the people in Hickory Hollow," Lena said when the pause in conversation grew awkward. "He diagnosed a young mother with appendicitis—"

Grandfather scowled. "He should be doing his job at Lakeview."

Lena broke off, sending Todd an uncertain glance at the interruption.

Maybe it was better to cut this short. Todd could apologize to Lena later, for inflicting his grandfather on her.

But he couldn't leave without finding out.

"I wanted to ask if you knew Alexander Huffman. Or anyone over at the department of health," Todd said. "The hospital certification for Lena's center is being held up and we can't get ahold of anyone who can help us push it through."

Grandfather's eyes narrowed. *Us.* Todd had said *us.* He saw the calculating expression on Grandfather's face. What was the older man thinking?

"I don't know anyone over there." Grandfather shifted in his seat. "Come talk to me later. Alone. It's time we got you back to the city."

It was a clear dismissal.

For the first time, Todd experienced a surge of frustration and anger toward his grandfather. Grandfather had tons of contacts in all aspects of the medicine world, thanks to a long illustrious career and a family legacy from his own father.

But Grandfather wasn't going to help.

Todd responded to Lena's gentle tug on his hand. They walked down to the edge of the lake, where the noise of lapping waves was more than that of voices chatting.

He let her go and ran his hand through his hair. "I'm sorry. I didn't think he'd be outright rude."

He saw the hurt she was trying to hide and his gut pitched.

Todd had let her down. It wasn't only his hopes that had crashed, but Lena's. He kicked at the soft sand beneath his feet. He wanted to throw something. Do something.

Lena wrapped her arms around her waist. "It's okay. I... I was thinking of gathering letters from families who've used the center. I may speak to Isaiah again. Find out if he will change his mind."

A letter-writing campaign. That seemed so old-fashioned. Would it even work?

There was a stubborn tilt to her jaw that might rival Grandfather's. "I won't give up."

He admired her determination.

A few months ago, he'd felt that way about working at the Lakeview ER.

But did he still feel the same now?

Maybe he needed to see it again. Just walking in the doors might spark his passion.

And he desperately needed some direction.

He smiled wryly. "Before we head back home, do you want to see where I'll be working? I'd love to show it to you."

Chapter Seventeen

"This is where the magic happens."

At Todd's words, Lena glanced around the interior of the hospital.

The building was six stories tall. Outside, she'd seen signage that there was a helicopter pad on the roof. Todd had escorted her through a set of automatic doors on the first floor just before an ambulance had pulled up with lights flashing.

Now they stood out of the way, in a sterile waiting room with tile floors and chairs that looked uncomfortable, roughly half of them filled with patients waiting to be seen. One man clutched his head, his elbows against his knees. He moaned. A little girl was crying next to her mother, who was bent over a clipboard of paperwork.

It was big and cold and the two women behind the standing desk at the far end of the room hadn't acknowledged any of the patients in the few minutes Lena and Todd had been standing here.

It was nothing like the clinic's welcoming atmosphere.

Todd seemed to be waiting on her to say something but Lena couldn't find words.

Since Henry's honest conversation and Todd's grandfather knocking the wind out of her with his coldness, she had been off-kilter.

She shouldn't have come. She should've stayed at home. But she'd wanted to see where Todd came from, what his life was like.

Now she had definitive proof that she didn't belong in it.

After the brief time with his grandfather, Todd had seemed almost determined to prove something. She just didn't know what.

"Doctor Barrett?" An older man with salt-and-pepper hair approached from the hallway that must lead to the exam rooms. He wore a white coat with a name badge clipped on the pocket.

In his dark slacks and button-up shirt, Todd would've looked the same, if he had a white coat. Todd had even clipped his name badge, taken from the dash compartment of his car, to his belt loop when they'd come inside.

"Lena, this is Doctor Elliott." Todd introduced her. "My new boss."

Doctor Elliott's curious gaze encompassed her and then moved back to Todd. "I was expecting you in two weeks."

Todd began to explain that they'd just stopped by for a brief visit, but she lost track of the conversation. Two weeks.

Until this morning, she'd thought of those two weeks as a chance to spend every spare moment with Todd. Soak up his affection, maybe steal a few more kisses.

She hadn't thought about how much it was going to hurt when Todd returned to his life in Columbus.

A nurse hurried down the hall and pulled Doctor Elliott aside, whispering what seemed to be an urgent conversation.

Todd turned to Lena, his hand closing over hers. It was a casual, affectionate touch, and the way their bodies were angled, no one else would be able to see it.

"Are you all right? You've been quiet this afternoon."

The concern in his expression threatened to loose the tears she could feel building in her throat.

Before she could answer, Doctor Elliott interrupted. "Excuse me, Doctor Barrett."

Todd let go of her hand and turned to his colleague.

"We've got a situation," Doctor Elliott said. "There's been a multicar accident and I've got several ambulances on their way to deliver critical patients. We sent one of our doctors home with a stomach bug earlier. Her replacement hasn't arrived yet. I could use your help."

Todd went into doctor mode. She felt the change in him immediately, the alertness and slight tension.

But he glanced at her and then back to his boss. "My start date—"

Doctor Elliott waved at the badge at Todd's waist. "As far as I'm concerned, you're already employed by the hospital. If someone from the legal team questions it, we'll tell them I brought you on as an independent contractor for a few hours. We need you."

Todd's expression showed how conflicted he was when he glanced at Lena again. "I can't just leave you alone."

Was he worried about her at this moment? It was sweet, but unnecessary.

She gestured to the waiting room, where someone was coughing so loudly it sounded as if it hurt.

"Your friend can wait in the doctor's lounge,

if you'd like." Doctor Elliott said the words before she could say the waiting room would be fine.

"It's fine." She tried to reassure Todd with a smile.

He escorted her to a room down the hall and around a corner.

"Are you sure you'll be all right?" Todd's hand under her elbow was warm.

"Of course. Go."

He brushed a kiss on her jaw and left her there in the quiet, empty room. The overhead lights seemed a bit too bright. She stood next to a round table with four chairs. Two vending machines buzzed from one wall. A fridge was next to them. A television was hung high on the wall in one corner. Two couches took up space against the other two walls.

She thought they'd passed a bathroom when they'd rushed down the hall. And her sudden need sent her scurrying to find it.

She was on her way back to the doctors' lounge when she passed by two wide double doors. The top half of the doors were actually windows and inside the triage room she saw Todd and several nurses working together, surrounding a small body on a gurney. A child.

From out here in the hall, she couldn't see

much of the patient on the bed. Only a leg and a hand. The child was still.

But she had a clear view of Todd. He wore an expression of confident determination. He was focused on the patient under his hands. He said something to the nurse standing to his right and the young man whirled away to grab supplies from the cabinet against a far wall. Another nurse took the first one's place, quickly leaning in to help as Todd said something to her.

Todd was in control. She had no doubt he would save the child whose life he held in his hands.

He was in his element, making snap decisions and controlling the action in the room. His attention never wavered from the patient under his care.

She stood and watched for a moment until the prick of tears in her eyes galvanized her to move. She returned to the doctors' lounge to find it still empty and quiet.

She sat on one of the couches and folded her hands in her skirt, crumpling the material in her fists.

Whatever vestiges of hope she'd had that Todd would want a life in Hickory Hollow were gone.

It couldn't be more obvious. He belonged

here. Saving lives. Working in this environment that made him light up. How could she have ever thought he would find contentment in their small town, with its quiet ways? It was fine for a diversion of a few weeks, but how could he ever be happy there in the long term?

They were too different, the two of them.

Now she knew.

Todd belonged here. And she didn't.

Todd stood in the corner of the ICU room, entering notes into the little boy's chart via computer. His fingers moved quickly over the keys. He glanced over at the bed, where the ten-year-old remained unconscious. But Todd and Doctor Elliott, who'd been in earlier to check on the boy, were hopeful.

Todd and his team had stopped an internal bleed and reset several bones.

Elation at the win remained at the back of his mind. Doctor Elliott had trusted him with the patient, and Todd had done everything he could to stabilize the boy. He'd felt confident in every decision. The team of nurses beside him had been competent and followed his leadership.

This was what he'd trained for, why he'd studied long hours and worked through a grueling residency.

But there was a part of him that felt...empty. Unsatisfied.

He couldn't make sense of it.

He finished his notes and signed out of the computer. The boy's mother was curled up in a chair next to the bed. Todd had thought she was sleeping, but when he passed by on his way out the door, he saw the glint of blue light reflecting off her face. She was on her cell phone. Maybe notifying other family?

She didn't even look up.

It had gotten late. Darkness had fallen outside the window as Todd had worked.

He wanted to thank the nursing staff who'd worked beside him. As he approached the nurses' station down the hall, he noticed two of the nurses he'd worked with in the treatment room, a man and woman.

The young man was clicking away at a computer, the woman had her nose glued to her phone. Neither were talking, chatting about their day.

Todd said a quick thanks, his gut roiling. He wasn't sure why.

His route to the lounge where he'd left Lena took him past the ER waiting room and he couldn't help scanning the patients from there. Some of them sat with eyes glazed as they watched the TV hung in one corner. Many of the others, even the children, were zoned out on their devices.

They were just like he'd been, before he'd stepped foot in Hickory Hollow. He'd been a slave to his technology. If his phone beeped or buzzed with a notification, he'd had to pick it up. The urge was too strong to deny. He'd received those tiny hits of dopamine by mindless scrolling of social media. Wasted so much time watching TV that he could've spent with the people he loved.

Maybe he was judging too harshly. The people in that waiting room were in survival mode. They needed help and were waiting for someone to see them.

But he couldn't shake the uneasiness that chased him down the hall.

He had arrived. He was two weeks away from stepping into his dream job. He'd gotten a taste of it tonight.

And something was missing.

He found that missing piece when he stepped into the lounge and caught sight of Lena. She was seated on one of the couches, reading a book.

She didn't register his presence and it gave him a moment to just soak her in. The soft curve of her jaw, the sweep of her lashes against her cheek, the spray of faint freckles across the bridge of her nose.

Lena wasn't just beautiful on the outside. She had a kind spirit. She was gentle and intelligent and compassionate.

And his life wouldn't be the same if she wasn't in it.

The realization knocked him back.

None of this meant anything without Lena by his side. Not the job, not the downtown apartment he'd once loved, not the busyness of a full social calendar.

He needed Lena.

She glanced up and blinked when she saw him standing there.

He had to clear his throat, the realization still sending shock waves through him. "Hey."

She closed the book on her lap. Motioned to a small shelf in the corner he hadn't noticed. "I borrowed this. I hope it's all right."

"I'm sure it's fine." Look at him. He could barely make basic conversation. He cleared his throat again to try and regain his equilibrium.

She put away the book and came to him. "How's your patient? Or patients?" But she didn't quite meet his gaze.

"Stable. There's a great team here to watch

over him." And Doctor Elliott reported that their staffing issue had been resolved. "You must be tired and hungry." He'd picked her up at the center early this morning to attend the reunion. And his stomach was grumbling that he'd missed dinner in the rush of saving a child's life.

She nodded, still not looking at him.

His stomach twisted. This time it wasn't about food. Something was wrong.

"Hey." He touched her waist and she jumped. "Are you…upset with me? I'm sorry for leaving you alone for so long." What had he been thinking? It wasn't like she could call an Uber and get a ride home. He'd basically trapped her here.

"No," she said softly. "Let's just go. I should get back to the center."

She wasn't telling him the truth. Or the whole truth. There was a wall between them, one that hadn't been there before.

He tugged her closer, sliding his arm around her waist. She rested with her shoulder against his chest, at an angle. He rested his chin on top of her head. It took a moment, but she finally relaxed against him.

He wished she'd tip her face up so he could see her. Or kiss her. But she kept her face averted. Something was going on.

His phone rang.

He was sorely tempted to ignore it, but Lena pulled away.

When he saw the Hickory Hollow area code, he answered immediately.

"Doctor Todd? This is Leroy Yoder. My wife, Priscilla, is having contractions. We came to the birthing center and the note on the front door said to call your number…"

Lena became alert as he asked a few questions and determined that Priscilla was in no imminent danger. When he mentioned that he and Lena were a good two hours from the center, the man insisted they would wait there.

He rang off, frowning. He would have rather the couple went on to the hospital instead of waiting.

"We have to get back," he told Lena.

Who seemed relieved that their conversation had been interrupted.

Chapter Eighteen

"You should lie down and rest for a while. I'll wake you if things progress." Lena said the words without looking up from where she scoured inside a lower cabinet.

She was in the middle of giving the center's kitchen a complete scrubbing. All the mixing bowls and pots from the cabinet were spread on the counter above her.

Work to keep her hands busy. To match her thoughts.

"You should rest, too," Todd said from where he stood just inside the kitchen.

"I'm fine," she insisted. "You should go and I'll call you when we need you."

She wasn't fine. She was exhausted, body and mind. She was heartsick.

Last night, she and Todd had rushed home

after receiving the phone call that Priscilla was in labor. They'd found her at the center with her husband and mother-in-law. She was indeed laboring…but things were moving slowly.

It wasn't unusual for a first-time mother. Hours had passed, and then the night had passed. Here they were, inching up on dawn and still no baby.

Priscilla's contractions were getting closer and closer. But it could be hours still.

All throughout the quiet night, Todd had been *right there*, making a pot of coffee, helping Lena make up a bed with clean linens, just being there with his reassuring and confident presence.

Lena couldn't stop thinking about him saving that child in the ER.

And she couldn't keep on pretending she was fine when her heart was breaking.

She needed space. And she wouldn't have that with him underfoot. She was going to ask him to leave until it was time.

Except, when she poked her head and shoulders out of the cabinet, he was moving between the fridge and stove. A skillet clanked as he placed it on the stovetop. In his other hand he had a carton of eggs that he placed on the counter.

"What are you doing?"

"Scrambling eggs." His answer was easy and casual. "I'm ravenous and you must be, too."

They'd only eaten a greasy drive-through hamburger as they'd raced home last night.

"Don't get too excited," Todd said. He concentrated on cracking the eggs into a bowl with the same gravity as if he was stitching up a patient. "Scrambled eggs are one of the three things I'm capable of cooking."

He was taking care of her. And it hurt, because she knew it wouldn't last.

"You mind handing me the salt and pepper?"

And when he glanced over his shoulder after the easygoing question, he must've caught sight of the emotions she'd couldn't hide any longer. A tear slipped down her cheek.

She turned and took a few steps to the kitchen nook, drawing in a deep breath and trying to steady her out-of-control emotions.

She heard him abandon the eggs on the counter, the quiet tread of his footsteps as he approached. "Lena?"

She knew she had to face this, face him. But when she turned and saw his dear face, she quailed. And when her voice emerged, it was unsteady. "I don't think we should spend any more time together."

She saw the brief crimp of his brows, the

confusion in his expression until her words registered. He *knew*. But he still asked, "What are you saying?"

"You belong in your emergency room," she said. "I saw it, last night. You were calm under pressure. You *thrive* on the pace of it. You lit up when you were helping that little boy. It's what you're supposed to do. Who you're supposed to be."

Another tear fell and she quickly whisked it away.

He watched the motion, and she saw his heart in his eyes. He reached for her.

But she stopped his touch with a staying hand. "Please, don't."

He dropped his hand. But then raised it again and rubbed the back of his neck. "Lena, I'm in—I care about you. Deeply."

His words only made the hole in the pit of her stomach deepen. She'd fallen for him—hard. No matter how many times she told herself she shouldn't, she couldn't seem to help it.

But she couldn't tell him. It would only make this more difficult.

"That's why we need to keep our distance, until your time here is up. We can't let this—" she gestured between them "—grow any more out of control."

His hand dropped to his side again. His eyes pleaded with her. "Lena, there has to be some way for it to work. For us to work. I've been trying to figure it out, but if you'd just help me—"

Her lips trembled and she pressed them together. "We both know you're going back to Columbus."

He shook his head wordlessly.

Hickory Hollow needs you. I need you.

But she didn't say the words that were making her throat ache. Because what she needed didn't change reality.

Todd's life had always been on a different trajectory from hers.

He moved, whirling to face the windows where the sun was just beginning to peek over the horizon. She remembered a morning together like this one, not so long ago. That other sunrise had been soaked with hope.

And now she was filled with despair.

Todd ran both hands through his hair, down his face. He made a noise that sounded just like she felt.

When he faced her again, she saw the raw emotion in his expression. "After last night, I don't know which way is up anymore." His voice was rough. "Ask me to stay."

His rough demand surprised her, confused her.

"Ask me to stay," he repeated. "And I will."

She swallowed hard as new tears pooled in her eyes. He cared about her that much? Enough to give up the life he'd planned, his job, his relationship with his grandfather?

She couldn't forget the tension she'd seen in him after he'd spoken to his grandfather. Or the intensity and confidence on his face when he'd been at the operating table.

"I can't," she whispered.

If she asked him to stay, if he gave up everything...then resented her? Resented a quiet life in Hickory Hollow? Or even worse...what if he stayed and discovered that she wasn't marriage material after all?

If she made the choice for him, it could ruin both of their lives. She couldn't.

A light flickered out in his expression. He seemed to steady himself, straighten his shoulders, but there was none of the warmth she'd grown used to in his eyes. "Okay."

A knock on the doorjamb startled them both.

It was Leroy. "She's saying the pain has changed. She wants to push."

Todd went into doctor mode. She saw the professional mask slip over him. She went to the sink to wash her hands and try to grab hold of her composure. She had none left.

But a baby was coming and it wasn't going to wait.

Later, she'd let out all the tears she hadn't been able to shed.

Todd stood next to his car in the bright mid-morning sunshine. Priscilla had borne a healthy baby girl, less than an hour after Todd's world had shattered at his feet.

Mother and baby were doing fine. Lena was bustling around the center, completing every-day tasks as if nothing was amiss.

As if it were only him who felt shattered.

He'd phoned Mrs. Smith earlier and asked her to push back his morning appointments. He knew there would be a line of patients waiting for him. He should get in his car and drive over to the clinic and get to work.

But he couldn't seem to stop staring at the ground stupidly. It wasn't only the exhaustion dogging him. His brain wouldn't stop exam-ining those moments in the kitchen, trying to figure out what he could've said or done to change things.

Lena didn't want to be with him.

He'd told her he cared about her. Told her that he would stay if she asked.

I can't.

Something didn't ring true to him in her rejection.

Or maybe that was wishful thinking.

He couldn't help but notice that she hadn't returned his declaration of feelings.

Maybe he'd been wrong about the whole thing.

No. No, he didn't believe that. Lena didn't have an untruthful bone in her body. She couldn't have faked the kisses they'd shared or the sparkle in her smile that was for him only.

He was going to march back inside and demand she—

What? Demand that she change her mind? Or maybe he could beg her to let him stay.

What was he even thinking?

The sound of tires on gravel grabbed his attention and shook him out of his swirling thoughts.

A black sedan with dark tinted windows turned into Lena's parking area. That looked like—

It was Grandfather's car. Todd barely covered his shock when his grandfather stopped right in the middle of the parking area—leaving no room for other cars or carriages to maneuver.

The driver's door opened and Grandfather got out. He rounded the car and approached Todd.

"You look terrible," were the first words out of the older man's mouth.

Todd looked down at the same slacks and shirt he'd worn to the reunion yesterday. So much had happened—he'd worn a borrowed pair of scrubs in the ER, then put these clothes back on. Late last night, he'd donned one of Lena's paper medical gowns over his clothes to welcome the new baby into the world. He looked rumpled and worn.

"It's been a long night," he told his grandfather. "What are you doing here? How did you find me?"

The old man scowled. "I shouldn't have to track you down. You should be in Columbus, doing your job. Your father told me where you'd be," he grumbled finally.

That didn't answer what Grandfather was doing here.

Todd's stomach twisted. In the wake of the emotional damage he'd taken this morning, he didn't have the bandwidth for a confrontation with Grandfather. And that's what he suspected the old man was here for.

"I can only talk for a minute," Todd said. "I have patients waiting for me at the clinic."

"You have a *job* waiting for you," Grandfather growled. "It's time to stop dillydallying in this podunk town and get to it."

Todd blew out a big breath. He didn't have time for this. "Doctor Elliott granted me the extension. I have two more weeks—"

Slicing his hand through the air, Grandfather interrupted him. "What do you think a hospital board is going to think about a hotshot like you who takes time off for make-believe volunteer work. That you're not focused. When it's time to choose the next chief of staff in a few years, you think they won't remember that you waffled on your start date?"

He was pretty sure Grandfather was exaggerating. Pushing back his start date by six weeks couldn't make that much of a difference to his career.

Thinking about a decade passing while he worked in the ER, without Lena at his side hurt. It was a physical ache.

"Grandfather—"

He didn't know what he was going to say. Maybe to ask his grandfather if they could table this discussion. Was this really why his grandfather had driven out in person two hours to see him?

But Grandfather didn't let him speak. "I want you at Lakeview by the end of the week."

That wasn't going to happen. Todd had made a commitment. And he was supposed to attend church with David and Ruby on Sunday morning.

"You've wasted enough time here—"

"It wasn't a waste." Todd spoke the words quietly, but they stopped Grandfather's rant.

It might've been the first time he'd ever spoken up against him.

"I've made a difference here," he said. He thought of little Randy. He might've died from that allergic reaction if Todd hadn't been present.

"I like it here," he went on. "I need some time to think. What if we were both wrong? What if family practice is what I'm meant for—"

Grandfather's face had turned an alarming shade of red. He pounded one fist on the trunk of his car. "You need to *think*? Boy, the only thing you need to consider is everything I've done for you."

Todd flinched. He wouldn't have made it through med school if not for Grandfather pushing him. And there'd been the scholarships and the connections...

"You come out here for a few weeks and now you're ungrateful for everything your grandmother and I sacrificed."

"I am grateful," Todd said quickly.

"Then act like it," Grandfather roared.

Grandfather had never spoken to him like that before. Todd blinked back sudden emotion that burned in his eyes.

Grandfather took a deep breath. When he spoke, his voice was lower. "You're a Barrett. That means something in Columbus and at Lakeview. You won't tarnish the family name by breaking a commitment we both made." Grandfather straightened his cuffs one by one. "I expect you back by the weekend." His repeated demand only made Todd itch to refuse.

"And if I'm not?"

Grandfather's eyes flashed. "Then you won't be my grandson anymore."

Todd knew it wasn't an idle threat. Not after Tyler.

Grandfather cuffed him on the shoulder. "I know you'll make the right decision. The only decision."

Chapter Nineteen

❦

"Onkle Todd!"

On another spring evening, the shrieks and giggles from his two nieces would've made Todd smile.

But tonight, as the girls raced across the yard toward him, his throat was closing up.

Todd approached the house on foot. David and Ruby were sitting on a pair of wooden rocking chairs on the porch, enjoying the warm, almost summer-feeling breeze. David said something to Ruby before he stood from his chair.

The sun was setting behind Todd. As he'd walked, the sky in front of him had become streaked with darker blues and purples. It must have been a beautiful sunset.

But he hadn't been able to turn around and appreciate it.

Mindy and Maggie raced up to him and threw their arms around his legs, threatening to topple him.

"Play with us, *Onkle* Todd!" Mindy cried. "I'm the horsey and Molly's the doggie. You can be the goat!"

He rested his palm on top of her head, careful not to dislodge the tiny prayer *kapp*. The place behind his nose burned. Grandfather wanted him to walk away from *this*.

Ungrateful.

Grandfather's unkind words had rattled through Todd's brain at different times throughout the day.

He was confused and heartsick. He wanted to talk to Lena about what had happened. Ask her advice.

But he couldn't.

After he'd wrapped up with his final patients at the clinic, later than usual, he'd walked down the street, toward Todd and Ruby's house.

Was he here to say goodbye?

David drew closer.

"I'm the bull and I say *Onkle* Todd can play with you in a bit." David's words were met with a chorus of giggles and Mindy let go of Todd's leg to dart across the lawn.

Maggie held on to his knee and tipped her

head back so she could look up into his face. "I love you, *Onka* Todd."

She couldn't know how her innocent words struck him right in the heart. His voice was rough when he said, "I love you, too, kiddo."

She gave him a toddler's snaggle-toothed grin and let go, following her sister with a shriek.

"Where is your car?" David asked.

"At the clinic."

David considered him. "For a moment, when I saw you walking up the road, I thought you were one of us."

One of us. He meant one of the Amish men in the community.

And his casual observation was like receiving a surgical incision with no anesthetic.

Todd must've made some noise or flinched or something because David's face shadowed with concern. "What's the matter?"

Everything.

"Grandfather surprised me with an in-person visit early this morning."

David motioned Todd to follow him, and they walked out to the front of the yard, away from the girls and their play. Ruby stayed on the porch.

Todd told him all about Grandfather's visit and his demands.

Maybe it was because David didn't know Grandfather, but he wasn't angry—or at least he didn't seem so—that Todd was supposed to leave early.

The sun wasn't finished with its brilliant display of colors. Todd ran out of words, watching the glowing orange ball slip toward the horizon. He couldn't feel the beauty of the moment. All he felt was empty. Empty and angry.

"What does Lena have to say?" David asked.

Todd wanted to howl at the pain unfolding inside him when he thought about Lena.

"She told me I belonged in Columbus." Todd choked out the words. "That was before Grandfather's visit. She said I should go home."

The same as Grandfather had.

Why was Todd so conflicted?

A buggy was coming up the road. David turned to look, and Todd used the moment to surreptitiously wipe his face. Maybe he shouldn't have come. He was sharing all of this with David, but what did he expect? For David to wave some magic wand and fix his life?

"I think that is John Riehl," David said.

The wagon slowed and stopped at David's drive.

Todd recognized the man, though he hadn't seen him in weeks. Tamara's husband had two little boys with him and they jumped out of the buggy and ran to join David's girls.

John walked over to David and Todd. "I'm glad to find you here," he said when he shook Todd's hand.

"How is Tamara?"

"She's well." John beamed. "The *boppli*, too. The little one is coming home in a few weeks."

Todd remembered Lena had told him the baby had been admitted to the NICU.

"That's *wonderbarr*," David said. "I know Ruby will want to send over a meal soon."

"Tell her thank you." John waved over David's shoulder to Ruby on the porch. Mindy had run up onto the porch and was showing her something in the palm of her hand.

John looked at Todd, his expression serious. "I haven't had time to stop by the clinic, so I'm glad to find you here tonight. Thank you. I'm so grateful for what you did for Tamara."

Todd shook his head, trying to refuse the sentiment. "I was only doing my job."

"You saved my wife's life. The baby, too. The surgeon said so."

Todd knew the dangers of an appendix rupturing, knew the complications when there was an unborn baby involved.

"I don't deserve any special thanks," he said.

"Well, I am thankful. To you and to *Gott*."

The conversation turned to a horse John needed shod and within moments, one of his boys ran up and claimed to be withering away from hunger. John took his leave.

David and Todd watched him load up in the buggy and go, waving as the horse pulled them down the street.

"She would have died, if you hadn't been here," David said quietly. His eyes remained on the buggy disappearing down the road.

"She might've died anyway," Todd said, though his argument lacked any real vigor. For the first time, he felt like he could talk about Elise Tanner. He told David everything. How nothing he'd been able to do had saved her.

He'd failed.

David rested one hand on Todd's shoulder. "You are a *goot* doctor. You will bless every patient that you treat, no matter where you work."

No matter where.

Todd's heart latched on to the thought of staying in Hickory Hollow. "Do you think I should stay?"

"What do you want to do?" Todd turned and looked him full in the face.

"I want to be with Lena." That answer came easily enough. He didn't even have to think about it.

"I want to be a part of the community here. A real part." Until now he hadn't thought about what it would mean to devote his life to the Amish church. But he'd started to feel a sense of belonging. And he wanted more of it.

"Even if it means giving up your car? And phone?"

Todd reached into his pocket, his hand automatically going for his phone—only to find it wasn't there. His empty pocket reminded him that he'd left it on his desk at the clinic. His subconscious was ready for this change.

"I don't need a car to be happy," he said. "Or a phone." He could visit with his parents more often. Convince Henry to come for a visit—somehow.

David considered him. "It would be a big commitment, to stay."

For the first time since Lena had pushed him away, Todd felt the tendrils of hope spreading through him. If he stayed, he could court Lena properly. Whatever he'd done that had made her push him away, he could fix it.

"I want to stay," he said, voice hoarse.

"Even if it means a break in your family—with your grandfather?"

The joy that was streaking through him tapered off. Here was the one block to his new plan.

Grandfather never would understand. Never would forgive him.

But was Todd going to live his life under Grandfather's thumb? Always following the plan someone else put in place for him?

Or was he man enough to make his own choices?

"Mr. Huffman?"

Lena pushed through the office door on wobbling legs even as she said the words.

The man behind the desk looked up, already frowning.

She'd made it this far. She wasn't giving up now.

She'd made this appointment with Alexander Huffman's office and had refused to take no for an answer.

She didn't recognize the older man, but he reminded her of a world-weary Todd from when she'd first met him.

Even that single, quick thought of Todd sent

a pang of loneliness and missing him through her. She took a deep breath and tried to expel it.

Behind her, Isaiah filed into the room.

Mr. Huffman's gaze skipped to him and he frowned fiercely. "What are you doing here?"

Lena was the one who spoke. "Mr. Huffman, I've brought all the paperwork for the birthing center. It's been double-and triple-checked. All it lacks is your approval."

He pressed one hand against his desk. "I won't approve it. Your center killed my daughter." His glare shifted to Isaiah, who'd gone tense beside her. "And you know it."

Lena reached out and touched Isaiah's wrist. It was a little presumptuous. They weren't friends. He'd reluctantly agreed to accompany her today, but she knew how difficult this had to be for him.

"That isn't true," Isaiah said, voice even. "Lena's center has helped dozens of mothers and babies."

Lena gestured to the sheaf of papers in her other hand. "I brought written statements from several of the women who have used the center in the past two years." She'd been touched when she'd read the handwritten missives. Each one described the care they'd received from Lena at the center and how it had made a wonderful, difficult time even better.

Each letter had solidified her mission. This was her calling.

"I don't need to see them," Mr. Huffman said. "I know how dangerous home births are." The words were said with a bitter twist to his mouth.

"Mr. Huffman, if you'd just give me a chance…"

But he was already shaking his head.

"I know there's no love lost between us." Isaiah said the words, his voice a little loud in the sudden silence in the office. "But Dorothy never stopped loving you." His hands were shaking. He had to clear his throat as emotion overtook him. "She was going to name him after you. The…the baby."

The older man flinched, turning to face the window.

"I know she wrote to you," Isaiah went on. "I don't know what you did with her letters. She would've come for a visit, if you would have invited her."

Mr. Huffman stared out the window, his eyes almost vacant. Was he even listening?

Lena's heart broke for this shattered relationship—and for Todd. Was this what it would've been like for him, if he'd chosen Hickory Hollow? If his grandfather had broken the family ties between himself and Todd?

She didn't want that for him.

"Losing Dorothy…and the *boppli*—it wasn't Lena's fault." Isaiah's voice was shaking. She was so thankful for him, for this moment. Helping her fight for the center even at the cost of his own grief. "Lena tried to convince Dorothy that a hospital birth was safer. More than once. Your daughter wouldn't listen."

Mr. Huffman did react to that, a quick glance at Lena. A questioning glance.

"The center has helped twenty-three mothers in the past year," she said. "And there were several that the doctor and I sent to the hospital. Some had underlying issues that meant it wouldn't have been safe for us to deliver. Some of them showed signs of distress in early labor."

"Dorothy wouldn't go," Isaiah said. "You know how stubborn she was."

"You should've made her," Mr. Huffman growled, his voice hoarse.

"Could you make her do anything she didn't want to do?"

The question was on the verge of being impertinent. Lena braced for Mr. Huffman to throw them out of the office.

But in his reflection in the glass, she saw a faint smile cross his lips.

"Lena does good work," Isaiah pushed.

Huffman sighed and turned back toward his desk. He looked worn. Still a grieving father. But when he glanced up, his expression had softened slightly. "I'll… I'll approve your registration."

Lena's heart leaped. He would?

She left the packet of papers on his desk where he indicated and quickly followed Isaiah from the building.

Moments later, they were ensconced in the back seat of the car they'd hired to bring them to the city today. Isaiah had his face averted, looking out the window on his side. She let him sit with his emotion, knowing that what he'd just gone through had to have brought his grief back to the surface.

She didn't know how to thank him.

She kept her eyes focused out her own window. She'd succeeded. The center would stay open. Mothers in Hickory Hollow would have access to the care they needed.

But the sense of victory was hollow.

She was hollow, a shell of herself.

She'd lost Todd. She'd given him up. She wouldn't regret it.

But when the car passed the same coffee shop where Todd had taken her that first morning when they'd gotten to know each other, her heart broke a little more. Tears pricked her eyes.

It turned out that her *mamm* had been wrong all those years ago. Lena *was* marrying material.

She'd just fallen for the wrong man.

Chapter Twenty

"It's a *goot* turnout," David said.

Todd stood with hands on his hips, surveying the groups of men gathered around the shell of the Lapp family's barn. A week ago, a fire had burned almost half of the structure. Today, the Amish community had turned out to tear down the ruined structure and rebuild it.

"*Goot* morning, Doc!"

Todd waved to one of the men as he called out a greeting in passing. He felt conspicuous in the homespun shirt and pants. And the suspenders…he was used to a belt. He rolled his shoulders under them, a tiny part of him afraid they were going to snap.

But he'd made a decision. One that felt right.

After a long discussion of what Todd might do to convince Lena he was here to stay, David had convinced Todd that consistent small gestures would mean more to her than any big gesture.

The next morning, Todd had met with the local bishop, David by his side. There'd been a long discussion of what it meant to join the Amish church, what the expectations would be for Todd.

Turned out, he was ready. Every moment since he'd arrived in Hickory Hollow had planted a seed of discontentment with his life the way it'd been before. Working alongside Lena and the folks of the community had watered those seeds until it had been necessary to make the change.

Todd had called and asked Mom and Dad to come down. They'd arrived a day later and he'd had a long talk with them, too. Mom wasn't surprised in the least. She'd exchanged a look with Dad that said everything.

But hearing about the big changes Todd was making in his life had prompted a deeper discussion of whether Todd could be happy living a simpler life in the long term—and what it might mean for the extended family.

Dad had promised to talk to Grandfather. Todd wasn't holding his breath that his grandfather would forgive him for making this change.

Todd had called his boss and explained everything. Doctor Elliott hadn't been happy. Todd had expected it, but the unkind words the man had said to him had been a blow.

Todd had wanted more than anything to share his emotions with Lena, but he hadn't spoken to her in a week—the longest they'd gone without speaking.

He missed her like a piece of himself was missing. He'd been busy this week, settling things with his old apartment and making the permanent move to Hickory Hollow on top of seeing patients daily.

And he'd been trying to give her time.

But he was really hoping to see her today.

"Do you think Lena will be here?" he asked his brother. He knew the work was going to start soon. An older man with a salt-and-pepper beard was beginning to give instructions to the men in groups closest to the barn.

"I don't know," David answered. "It's possible."

They were pulled onto a work crew, and Todd couldn't help glancing around the women setting out food on long tables set up away from the barn.

The cool of the morning wore off soon enough as they worked. Todd started to sweat under the exertion. Still no Lena, but he was pulled off the work crew to stitch up a teen boy who had cut the fleshy part of his arm on a protruding nail.

He sent the young man's friend to grab his black bag from David's buggy and sat the boy on one of the benches near where the women were setting out food, putting a hand to the teen's shoulder when he went pale and threatened to faint.

He was almost done with the needle and thread when he heard her dear voice.

"Todd?"

He put in the last stitch and glanced up to find Lena staring at him, wide-eyed, from several yards away.

His heart leaped.

"Hey," he said far more casually than he felt. He had to look back at the boy's arm to tie off his surgical thread.

In his peripheral vision he saw that Lena seemed frozen to the spot.

He patted the teen on the shoulder. "Come into the clinic tomorrow for a tetanus shot. It's important."

The teen nodded and rushed away.

And Todd was left with his stomach knotted and heart pounding in his ears.

He peeled off the sterile gloves he'd donned

and tucked them into a small disposable bag. He used a disinfectant wipe to clean his hands and the tabletop and then tucked it away, too, to be disposed of later.

And then he stood up and faced her.

Her eyes raked him from head to toe. He saw the confusion in her expression.

"What are you doing here?" she murmured. She stepped closer.

"I'm helping." He waved to the barn. "I was pounding nails in the south wall just before I got waylaid."

"But what are you doing *here*?" Was he imagining that hopeful tone in her voice? Surely not.

"I—"

"Todd!" A bellow carried across the field in front of the barn.

He recognized that voice. Grandfather.

Dread crashed over him in a tidal wave. He turned to see his grandfather marching across the yard, ignoring the shocked murmurs and stares of everyone in his wake.

Todd moved to intercept him. He was aware of Lena following behind him. He wished she had stayed away. He could guess what Grandfather was going to say, and it wasn't going to be pretty.

"Boy, I'm not going to let you throw away your life."

"I'm not throwing my life away." He reached out to take Gramps's arm, but the older man shook him off.

"You quit the hospital before your first day and I have to hear about it from Elliott?"

Lena's sharp intake of breath came behind him.

"Can we talk about this somewhere more private?"

Grandfather was worryingly red-faced. "No. We'll talk about it now. You can't quit your job, and you can't give up the legacy our family strove for to move to a dead-end job in this podunk town."

Lena heard the words from Todd's grandfather. She'd been stunned to see Todd here dressed as an Amish man.

Perhaps her mind had refused to believe what her eyes and ears were telling her until this moment, when Todd said, "I *am* staying."

There were still things left unsaid between them. But at this moment, none of that mattered.

She took the step that brought her even with Todd and slipped her hand into his.

He glanced at her briefly, his eyes filled with gratefulness and warmth. When he spoke to his grandfather again, his voice was even. "Working alongside the people of Hickory Hollow is my calling. I am taking steps to join the Amish church, and I'll practice medicine here as long as they'll have me."

Todd's grandfather seemed to deflate the slightest bit. There was still anger in his voice when he said, "If that's your choice, I disown you. You aren't welcome in my house. I won't speak to you again. You are cut out of the inheritance I will leave behind. You are nothing to me. Less than nothing."

Todd flinched at the terrible words.

Her other hand joined the first in squeezing Todd's. "Your grandson isn't nothing," she said passionately. "He has already saved lives and he is needed here. You should be proud of him."

The older man's gaze dismissed her and the way she was holding on to Todd.

"Don't come crawling to me when you find out this life isn't for you. You're a Barrett. You're not meant for this."

The words were an echo of what she'd once believed about Todd. How could someone like him be happy here in this sleepy little town? How could he be content with her?

Todd's chest expanded as he took a slow, deep breath. "I'm right where I belong."

His words were like water on a parched garden inside her heart. For the first time since she'd pushed him away, hope swirled inside her.

Todd's grandfather shook his head. Underneath his anger, he looked sad. And old. He turned to go, muttering something under his breath that Lena couldn't hear.

Todd watched him go, and she watched Todd. Noticed the fine lines bracketing his eyes, the tension in the set of his jaw.

It had to be incredibly difficult, watching his grandfather walk away angry. There'd been no real resolution between them, only angry words from his grandfather's side and a calm decisiveness from Todd.

And then Todd was turning slightly toward her, their clasped hands between them. Some of the tension drained from him and his eyes softened.

"Hi," he said.

"Hi." Her heart was his, and at the gentle look in his eyes, it opened like a flower blooming in the bright spring sunlight.

A sudden realization came over his expression as he took in their surroundings. She was already aware of the curious stares they were drawing from neighbors and friends.

"When I pictured us finally having a chance to talk, I didn't imagine such a big audience."

His words made her smile. He'd imagined this moment? She hadn't. She hadn't dared to dream…

"Maybe we could go somewhere," she suggested. "Just for a bit. Is your car…?"

One corner of his mouth tipped in a wry smile. "Sold. David drove me in his buggy."

He'd sold his car? This was serious.

"Maybe we could take a walk," he said.

"Yes."

Todd didn't let go of her hand as they skirted several of the buggies and slipped away from the noise of the workers raising the barn.

Todd glanced over his shoulder. "David will probably give me a hard time for slipping away."

"Brothers are good at teasing like that."

They didn't go far, stopping by the side of the road underneath a sturdy oak tree.

Todd let go of her hand, only to turn and face her. "I wanted—"

"I'm sorry," she blurted, speaking at the same time.

He motioned for her to go first.

"I can't believe you're here. I—" She laughed

a little breathless laugh. "*Why* are you here? I can't believe it…"

Tears were pooling in her eyes.

Todd gave a little groan and tugged her into a hug. It was relief and joy to be held in his arms. She pressed her cheek against his broad shoulder as a sense of coming home settled inside her.

"I spent most of last weekend with David, talking through things. What kind of life changes I would have to make to stay. My parents came up for an afternoon. Grandfather doesn't understand, but they get it." There was a smile in his voice, as if he was thinking about an inside joke shared between him and his parents. "I even spent several hours with the bishop. There are some things still up in the air, but… I'm here for good."

She edged back slightly so she could see his face. "It certainly seems as if you've thought of everything. What is there left to do?"

He raised one hand to cup her jaw. "I wanted to see you. From the instant my decision was made. David convinced me I should wait."

"I'm sorry for sending you away," she whispered. "I wanted to ask you to stay, but I…" She inhaled a choppy breath that hurt her throat. Let herself be vulnerable. "I was afraid. To ask you to choose me."

He smiled slightly as a single tear slipped down her cheek. He brushed it away with the pad of his thumb. "I choose you," he whispered. "And I choose myself. I like who I can be here in Hickory Hollow. It turns out I'm someone who finds peace in the simple things."

Joy overflowed in her heart and those last little questions she'd held—was his grandfather right, would he resent her in a year or two or ten?—slipped away.

Todd had chosen this.

"Is there anything else?" she asked.

He nodded, expression gone serious. "I can't live with the Schrock family forever. I'll need something more permanent. I don't want to build something, though. Not if there's a place for me, beside you."

Breath caught in her chest. Was he saying…?

He brushed his thumb along her jaw. "Lena, I love you. I've loved you since that first moment I walked through your door. You've kept me on my toes, challenged me, listened to me, shared your heart with me. I love you," he repeated in a whisper.

Joyful tears fell. "I love you, too," she whispered.

He kissed her tears away, brushing gentle touches of his lips against her cheeks.

"You've changed me—for the better. Made me believe in myself, hope for the family I thought I would never have. I love you," she repeated, just before his lips covered hers in a tender kiss.

When he broke the kiss a moment later, he inhaled a shaky breath. "So does this mean… Will you marry me?"

She laughed a little, brushing the remains of joyful tears from her cheeks. "You don't want a long courtship before you ask?"

He narrowed his eyes at her. "Do you?"

"No." She'd waited long enough for a husband of her own.

Chapter Twenty-One

"Is that better, *Aendi* Kate?"

Lena asked the question as she finished rubbing her *aendi's* right foot. Minutes ago, she'd made the bed with new sheets. She'd brought fresh flowers with her upstairs to fill the vase on the windowsill.

Aendi Kate had relaxed under her ministrations and her head came up from where it had lolled back against the rocking chair.

"You are a *goot* girl, Lena. *Danke*."

She stood and smoothed a wrinkle out of the quilt that topped the made bed on her way out of the room.

She was on the stairs when she heard the murmur of voices from the kitchen doorway. She paused on the fourth step from the bottom, listening.

"Lena will be down in a bit." That was *Mamm's* voice and there was a lower murmur that Lena couldn't make out.

"I can make a bed as well as anyone." That was Todd's dear voice. "She was up half the night managing a birth—"

His voice was close, and she saw one dark shoe and the hem of his pant leg through the doorway, as if *Mamm* had stopped him there, on his way to the staircase.

"Lena didn't tell me she'd been up all night."

"Of course she didn't."

Her husband's—months later, it still filled her with wonder to think the words—voice was almost argumentative.

Todd had settled into the Plain life with only a few small hiccups. He got along well with her parents. *Mamm* had been surprised and delighted by their wedding announcement. *Daed* had been silent and watchful.

Lena's sisters had been ecstatic. Almost as much as she had been.

Todd was well liked in the community, and respect for him continued to grow. His practice was thriving. And she got to work alongside him if their schedules aligned.

"Lena always thinks of others first," Todd

said, interrupting the happy thoughts that had stayed her feet on the stairs. "I'll just go help—"

"There's no need," she called out to him. "I'm finished."

He popped through the doorway, holding a black wool coat over one arm.

His beard—a sign to everyone that he was a married man—had come in and made him more handsome.

His eyes lit up when he saw her.

She descended the last few steps and joined him at the landing. He clasped her hand beneath the coat he held, and only for a moment, before letting her go.

Her people didn't often make public displays of affection. But that one touch was enough to soothe the slight tension she felt at being away from him for the evening.

"You didn't have to come all this way to fetch me," she said as she passed into the kitchen.

He followed. "I wanted to. It's dark already."

His gentle protectiveness warmed her.

This dinner with her parents had been planned for several days. Earlier, he'd called the center to let her know a patient with a badly broken arm had come in late in the day and he wouldn't make it to supper. She'd come anyway, happy to see her parents and her *aendi*.

The bishop and other church leaders had made some allowances in technology for Todd's clinic, though he'd given up his cell phone and car.

He didn't seem to miss the objects. His parents visited frequently and Todd and Lena were busy and happy. They spent a lot of time with David and Ruby and their family.

She gave *Mamm* a brief hug. "*Aendi* Kate is all settled. *Danke* for dinner."

Mamm hugged her back. When she pulled away, her eyes were suspiciously moist and she sniffled.

"What's the matter?" Lena asked.

Mamm swiped under her eyes with a little laugh. "Nothing. I'm just so pleased to see you happy. Soon enough, you'll have a house full of little *bopplies.*"

Lena gave her *mamm* another hug. "If *Gott* wills it."

Over her mother's shoulder, she caught Todd's eye. She'd shared with him about the long-held tensions between the two of them. During the past months, she'd been able to forgive *Mamm* and move past old hurts.

He smiled at her. They'd talked about starting a family. They both wanted children, though it would mean she might need to hire someone to help with the center. In time. Everything in *Gott's* time.

She separated from *Mamm*, and Todd held out her coat. She slipped her arms inside, a pulse of warmth beating inside her at the brief clasp of his hands on her shoulders.

And then they left, bundling up in the closed buggy.

Todd was quick to claim her hand.

"Everything all right at the clinic?" she asked.

"Yes. I missed you."

When the center didn't need her, she'd begun helping more, sometimes even when Mrs. Smith was present. It meant more time together.

"I can't wait to be home," Todd went on.

Her heart warmed. *Home.*

Living at the center was both different and the same as before. Having a partner there to share chores. Todd always on hand in case she needed his medical opinion. Shared smiles over the breakfast table. The little surprises he sometimes left for her, like this morning's gift of a book she'd mentioned in passing weeks ago.

She'd never been so content. How was this her life?

Gratefulness settled over her as she snuggled close to her husband.

* * *

"Oh, Jenny has a booth for her quilts. I want to go look."

Todd indulged Lena and followed her down the wide walkway of the farmers' market on Saturday morning, a few days after he'd picked her up after dinner at her parents' house.

Lena browsed the quilts folded neatly on long tables, chatting with Jenny while Todd stood near the booth's edge.

The autumn morning was crisp and sunny. The leaves had turned over the past two weeks, and walking along any of the streets in Hickory Hollow was a colorful experience.

"Doc Barrett!" A young mother approached with a baby in her arms and two little ones in tow. Jane Glick. The first mother whose baby he'd delivered here.

He always went on alert when he heard his name. He quickly glanced over the young mother, then at her children in turn. He couldn't see any visible injuries or sickness. His bag was in the buggy, not far from here, if he needed it.

"Good morning," he greeted them.

"*Goot* morning," the children echoed quietly. The boy and girl both stared up at him curiously.

"Little Tommy here told me just the other

day how he wanted to grow up and become a doctor, like you."

Todd felt a faint blush heat his neck and jaw.

The little girl tugged on her mother's skirt. "My boots came untied," she whispered.

Jane frowned, the wheels in her mind obviously turning. It would be difficult to juggle tying the shoes while holding a baby. And there was nowhere out here to put the baby down.

"Here. I can take her for a minute," he offered.

The grateful mother handed him the baby, swaddled in a blanket. He'd thought the little one was asleep, judging by how quiet she was, but she looked up into his face with wide, hazel eyes.

The baby cooed and his heart squeezed.

At that moment, Lena glanced over from the quilt she was looking at. Her expression softened and his heart responded. After her mother's comments, they'd spent a long time after the buggy ride home, talking and dreaming about what it would be like to start their own family.

He couldn't wait.

He'd never dreamed he would be so content here, but he was.

"Thank you, Doc." Jane took her sweet baby back and she and the children said goodbye.

Todd was waving at the little boy as he walked off with his mother when he caught sight of a familiar man dressed in a pair of jeans and sweatshirt. The clothing had drawn his eye, as out of place as it now seemed to Todd.

But he recognized the man.

Henry.

What was his brother doing here?

Watching him, that much was clear. Henry had his hands in his pockets and was staring straight at Todd.

Lena joined him, sliding her hand into the crook of Todd's elbow. "I'm finished admiring the quilts. Are you hungry…?"

Her question trailed off as she glimpsed Henry, who was crossing the space between them.

Her hand flexed on Todd's arm. She knew how badly he wanted reconciliation with his brother. Henry had come to their wedding, sat next to Mom and Dad. He'd barely said a word to Todd and had left before the traditional wedding lunch was shared.

But Todd could forgive all of that. Henry was here.

Henry's steps slowed when he neared.

But Todd closed the final distance between them, letting Lena's hand slip away, to pull his brother into a hug.

"I'm so glad to see you," he said.

Some emotion glittered behind Henry's eyes when they parted. Henry shoved his hands back in his pockets. He nodded to Lena, who came to stand at Todd's side.

"Hello, Henry. It's *goot* to see you."

"What are you doing here?" Todd asked.

Lena nudged his side and he laughed a little.

"I didn't mean that like it sounded. I'm happy to see you. It's just unexpected."

Henry glanced away. A muscle ticked in his jaw before he sighed.

"Did you really mean what you said, back in April?"

Todd shook his head. He'd left his brother multiple voice mails back then, sent so many emails. He'd been discovering what he'd missed in his climb to be the doctor he thought he should be—and realized it was his brother. "I said a lot of things. And I meant them all."

Henry looked back at Todd. His gaze slipped to Lena then back.

Intuitive as ever, she squeezed Todd's arm. "I see a friend. I'll be back."

She walked away, giving them a bit of privacy in the busy space.

Henry sighed. "You said you missed how we used to be. Playing basketball and talking about girls."

Those days were long ago. But Todd did miss the closeness they'd shared. The sense of them against the world.

"I haven't been a good brother," Todd said. "I let go of my relationship with you to chase a dream it turned out I didn't even want. I'm sorry."

Henry considered him for a long moment. "I'd like to try to rebuild. With you."

Todd's heart leaped with joy. He'd prayed for this moment. "Yes. Of course, I want that." He thought for a second. "I can hire a car and come up to the city some weekends."

Henry shook his head. Not good enough?

"Weeknights are hard," he thought aloud. It was such a long drive that it wouldn't give them much time together.

"No, that's not what I meant." Henry shifted his feet. "I—" Now he looked the tiniest bit sheepish. "I bought a house here. To flip," he added quickly. "It's in terrible condition, but give me a couple of months of renovations…"

"You're staying for a few months?" Excitement poured through Todd.

"Yeah."

"This is great. You can come to breakfast at David and Ruby's. I know the girls would love to get to know you—"

But Henry was shaking his head. "I don't— David isn't my brother. You are. I'm here for you."

Todd's insides knotted, but he forced a smile. "I want to be close again."

But there was a part of him that had also wanted the impossible—for Henry and David to become true brothers, for that relationship to find healing, too.

Nothing was impossible with God, was it? Just look at him.

He and Henry spoke for a few more minutes, promising to meet for coffee one morning this week before Todd opened the clinic.

When Henry left, Lena came back almost immediately.

"Henry is renovating a house in Hickory Hollow." He said the words, even though he still couldn't truly believe them.

"He is? That's *wonderbarr*!"

From the way her face was lit up, he knew she really meant it.

"I love you," he said quietly, not wanting to share this moment with everyone around them. New realization stole over him. "I love you more and more every day."

She blushed a little, but her eyes were shining as she looked up at him. "I love you, too."

He had come to Hickory Hollow to help, to get to know his long-lost brother. He'd never expected to find love here, to meet Lena.

But God had other plans for him. Better plans.

And Todd couldn't be more thankful.

* * * * *

*If you liked this story from Lucy Bayer,
check out these previous
Love Inspired books:*

A Convenient Amish Bride
by Lucy Bayer

Her Amish Adversary
by Vannetta Chapman

The Mysterious Amish Nanny
by Patrice Lewis

*Available now from Love Inspired!
Find more great reads at
www.LoveInspired.com.*

Dear Reader,

Thank you for reading *Their Forbidden Amish Match*. Some author friends helped me with the brainstorming for this book, including Todd's first moments in Hickory Hollow—when he steps in something he shouldn't. Making Todd uncomfortable was one of the things I liked most about writing this book. His journey of discovery was refreshing to me, and a good reminder to slow down and enjoy the little everyday miracles God blesses us with. I hope you see God's hand working in your life today and every day. God bless, and thank you for reading.

Lucy Bayer